DEATH OVER DEATH

Villareal's eyes flicked over Marten's face, then back to the body, still obscenely illuminated by the harsh television lights. "I am going back—come in my car. We can discuss what information to release. Alvalos," he beckoned to the round-faced young officer. "Take the lieutenant's keys, and bring his car to the station."

The agent scooped up the keys with a grin, and Marten explained where the car was parked.

Villareal seemed in no hurry to move. "If this is not the Strangler's work, everyone must be told this at once. So we will concentrate on that. But I have something to—"

"Lieutenant, Lieutenant, you've forgotten your notebook."

Marten turned and saw Alvalos hurrying back toward the lighted area, a black clipboard notebook held out at arm's length. He waved it, his youthful face reflecting his pleasure in being helpful.

The flash of light from the notebook's explosion was brighter than the television lights. Alvalos' body was hurled backwards and lay still. . . .

Bantam Books offers the finest in classic and modern American murder mysteries. Ask your bookseller for the books you have missed.

Stuart Palmer

THE PUZZLE OF THE SILVER PERSIAN
THE PUZZLE OF THE HAPPY HOOLIGAN

Craig Rice

MY KINGDOM FOR A HEARSE
HAVING WONDERFUL CRIME

Rex Stout

AND FOUR TO GO
BAD FOR BUSINESS
THE BROKEN VASE
DEATH OF A DUDE
DEATH TIMES THREE
DOUBLE FOR DEATH
A FAMILY AFFAIR
THE FATHER HUNT
FER-DE-LANCE
THE FINAL DEDUCTION
GAMBIT
THE LEAGUE OF FRIGHTENED MEN
MURDER BY THE BOOK
NOT QUITE DEAD ENOUGH
PLOT IT YOURSELF
THE RED BOX
THE RUBBER BAND
SOME BURIED CAESAR
THE SOUND OF MURDER
THREE DOORS TO DEATH
THREE FOR THE CHAIR
TOO MANY CLIENTS

Victoria Silver

DEATH OF A HARVARD FRESHMAN
DEATH OF A RADCLIFFE ROOMMATE

William Kienzle

THE ROSARY MURDERS

Richard Fliegel

THE NEXT TO DIE

M. J. Adamson

NOT TILL A HOT JANUARY

Max Byrd

CALIFORNIA THRILLER
FINDERS WEEPERS
FLY AWAY, JILL

R. D. Brown

HAZZARD

Sue Grafton

"B" IS FOR BURGLAR

Robert Goldsborough

MURDER IN E MINOR

Ross MacDonald

BLUE CITY
THE BLUE HAMMER
GOODBYE LOOK
THE MOVING TARGET

A. E. Maxwell

JUST ANOTHER DAY IN PARADISE

Rob Kantner

THE BACK-DOOR MAN

Joseph Telushkin

THE UNORTHODOX MURDER OF RABBI WAHL

Ted Wood

LIVE BAIT

Barbara Paul

KILL FEE
THE RENEWABLE VIRGIN

Benjamin M. Schutz

EMBRACE THE WOLF

S. F. X. Dean

DEATH AND THE MAD HEROINE

NOT TILL A HOT JANUARY

M. J. Adamson

BANTAM BOOKS
TORONTO · NEW YORK · LONDON · SYDNEY · AUCKLAND

NOT TILL A HOT JANUARY
A Bantam Book / January 1987

ISBN 0-553-26201-7

Published simultaneously in the United States and Canada

Bantam Books are published by Bantam Books, Inc. Its trademark, consisting of the words "Bantam Books" and the portrayal of a rooster, is Registered in U.S. Patent and Trademark Office and in other countries. Marca Registrada. Bantam Books, Inc., 666 Fifth Avenue, New York, New York 10103.

PRINTED IN THE UNITED STATES OF AMERICA

O   0 9 8 7 6 5 4 3 2 1

To Dan, I dedicate half this book;
the other half is surely your own.

LEONATO: You will never run mad, niece.
BEATRICE: No, not till a hot January.

Much Ado About Nothing

ACKNOWLEDGMENTS

All the men and women that I spoke to at Police Headquarters in San Juan, Puerto Rico, were knowledgeable and extraordinarily accessible. My special thanks to Investigator Irving Lugo of the Homicide Section and to Ed Poullet, a real expert in public relations. Dr. C. W. Reiquam of the Pathology Department at Denver's Presbyterian Hospital generously provided me with scientific information. Mistakes in reporting are mine.

I am very grateful to Dr. Elspeth MacHattie for her careful reading, and to Jane Gelfman and Deborah Schneider at John Farquharson for all their encouragement *and* services. It was my extreme good fortune to have Kate Miciak at Bantam Books as my editor.

1

THE FLASHLIGHT'S POWERFUL beam moved slowly up
past the delicate arch of the foot, along the curve of the
tanned calf and thigh, and then wobbled and stopped.
Across the girl's naked buttocks, there was an unmistakable
triangle of white, once protected by a bikini. Officer Hernandez felt weak-kneed. His light caught the glint of gold
rings on her outstretched right hand, then slid across her
shoulder and another strip of white from a shoulder strap.
Her face was half-hidden in the soft sand, but one light eye
bulged open. Her hair was short and very blonde.

Reaching and feeling gingerly for a pulse, he almost
stumbled in his haste to back up, to avoid leaving his own
prints. He steadied himself against the fender of his blue
and white police car with the *Tránsito* symbol emblazoned
on the door. He closed his eyes for a long moment. He
opened them and aimed his flashlight ten feet to the right.
The body was still there. The only coherent thought he had
was that the girl was probably not Puerto Rican. There
would be much trouble.

He had only one quick thought of pain for the lifeless girl. Officer Hernandez was himself a most compassionate man, but his superior officer was decidedly not. *Policía de Tránsito* Captain Miguel Padilla had himself come up through the ranks as a traffic patrolman, but his insistence on strict adherence to rules was almost legendary.

Especially lately. There had already been so much trouble for the *Policía*.

Tomorrow, Hernandez thought hopelessly, the captain would sit in his crisply pressed uniform and stare grimly at his sweat-stained subordinate. He would icily inquire why Hernandez was parked on the edge of San Juan Bay at 11 P.M. when the traffic he was responsible for was some distance away on the Bayamon Loop Highway.

It would then have to be told: his regular stops at Juanita's Restaurant each night, where a warm, flaky empanadilla and two bottles of chilled and carefully wrapped Heinekens were always handed to him by the cheerful owner before she closed. He would even have to confess that it was the Dutch beer which he himself could seldom afford.

Then the Captain would begin to shout, would even switch to English, which Hernandez was supposed to know as a condition of his job, but which he would forget in his embarrassment. It would do no good to mention that all the restaurant owners gave the police free meals, that a very little break, to eat, to stare at the lighted cruise ships on the horizon, to stretch one's legs, to relieve oneself in the murky water, was in the course of nature.

The Captain would not have to remind him, but he surely would, that the death of a continental American would require an intensive investigation. That the body of this girl would not just be a paragraph in the Police Blotter section of the *San Juan Star*, but a bold, black headline on the front page and worse, a screaming red headline in *El Clamor*. That although other women's bodies were found floating in the Bay, *they* had been put there by enraged husbands or boyfriends who were easily traced by the police.

The Chief would point out to him, in withering detail, that this case would attract crowds of reporters begging the Homicide Department for new information. That the Homicide Department would be irritated beyond measure because they would have nothing to tell because a police car's tire tracks had covered vital clues; that a traffic policeman's big, clumsy footprints were all up and down the beach. That the Puerto Rican press was remorseless; that Officer Hernandez would be interviewed. His wife would even be interviewed. But what was worse, much much worse, the image of the Puerto Rican police would again be tarnished and that he, Captain Miguel Padilla, would have to admit that his own *Tránsito* force was being bribed with crab pies and imported beer!

Reaching for the mike on his dashboard, Officer Hernandez tried desperately not to think of the morning.

At that moment, in another part of San Juan, Herman Villareal, Chief of that same Homicide Department that would so soon bring misery to Officer Hernández, was himself dodging certain thoughts. His also concerned a dead girl. But she was not the same girl that the traffic patrolman was eyeing with such anxiety. Villareal did not know about her. It would be a while yet before his phone rang.

On the other hand, Villareal knew *all* about Teresa Casera. She was definitely Puerto Rican. She had been dead for two months. Someone had put a knee in her back and a stick against her throat. The knee had forcibly pushed her soft neck against the hard stick, which had been tightly held by a man's two hands, one on each end. Her larynx and trachea had been crushed. It was an efficient way to kill. She had died quickly and quietly. The stick had most probably been a police nightstick.

For that crime, two uniformed Puerto Rican policemen had been indicted and were waiting trial. One had almost certainly murdered the girl. The other had probably been chatting with Teresa at the time.

Teresa spent a great deal of time in the company of police officers. She was a police groupie.

She was there when certain officers boasted about stores they had robbed while in uniform. She was there when they mentioned the packets of cocaine they had picked up at drug busts but had not turned in. She delivered the cocaine to a drug dealer named Luis the Cricket, who had paid her well. And she had faithfully carried the money back to those policemen. She was even pregnant by one of the officers, although no one, including Teresa, was exactly sure which one.

She had not been a particularly intelligent girl. But she had known a lot. And she had talked a lot. Too much.

For weeks, the Casera case had dominated the headlines. Journalists had besieged the Police Department. The Puerto Rican Justice Department, charged with investigating corruption in other government agencies, had beleaguered the Police Department. It was the most difficult of times for Puerto Rico's ten thousand policemen, particularly for the vast majority of those officers who had not robbed, perjured, or murdered and whose job, at the best of times, was a hard one.

Villareal's own Homicide One Squad had not been directly implicated. Some of the detectives had been closely questioned, but none of the evidence uncovered had pointed to them.

Villareal continued looking at the large stack of administrative paperwork in front of him, an activity that filled his solitary evenings and almost always soothed him. But now he fidgeted, running his hand over his thinning hair, smoothing his mustache. He shook his Chiclet box for another piece of gum. It was empty. He groped around his desk for the cigarettes for some time before he remembered he'd given up smoking.

He stopped staring at the statistics and thought over what he knew of one detective's connection with Teresa Casera. The man's name was Angel Negrón. Because of his macho reputation, his large network of fearful informers, Negrón was much admired by some of the younger uniformed officers, including some of those who had been summarily dismissed from the force at the time of the Casera investigation. He had even been seen by several witnesses in bars with the two indicted policemen.

Negrón was experienced. In some respects, his record was impressive. But his methods caused concern. He had twice been suspended for investigation of police brutality. Each time, the charges had been dropped. He was due back at Homicide One on Monday morning.

Villareal stared at the wall ahead of him. The thought of Negrón persisted like a fly on a hot June morning. If there was any further trouble—and it should leak out . . . Villareal felt his own neck edgily. What if he just transferred him? Negrón could be sent to Homicide Two.

Villareal sighed. No. One could not cover up the sky with one's hand. Negrón was his responsibility. And in Homicide Two, the possibility for trouble would be even greater. Homicide Two worked on the murder cases where the killer was known or strongly suspected. Confessions were very desirable. There Negrón might be even more likely—

The ringing of the phone startled him. It was almost midnight. Picking up the receiver, he heard the agitated, exasperated voice of Captain Miguel Padilla of the *Tránsito Policía*.

New York Police Lieutenant Balthazar Marten had become adept at not thinking of certain subjects. Since a year ago this January. Now, as he stared at the terminal building at JFK Airport through the snow-streaked window of the 747, he tried to distract himself, as always, by focusing on the details of his work. But he had been told little about his new assignment. He hadn't liked what he'd heard.

He was being sent to Puerto Rico. He did not want to go to Puerto Rico. Moreover, he was a homicide detective and this was not a homicide case.

The Puerto Rican *Policía* had requested the help of an officer experienced in gambling and its link with organized crime. A new casino had recently opened on the Condado, the tourist section of San Juan. It was suspected that drug dealers, always eager to find additional ways to launder their money, might be involved. He would be fully briefed on arrival.

Surprisingly, the information about his new assignment had been given to him by the Commissioner himself, while Captain Helmsley, his own immediate superior, sat quietly at Balthazar's side. Helmsley had even been wearing a new shirt. Most New York policemen only saw the Commissioner in newspaper photos, smiling reassuringly at the public, or from the backs of crowded halls. It was, however, the third time that Balthazar Marten had met him.

The first time, eighteen months before that, under the hot lights of television cameras, the Commissioner had given him a warm handshake and a commendation for his work on the River Rat case. "We, as members of a civilized society," the Commissioner had then intoned, "cannot tolerate those men who, like beasts of prey, stalk and kill. We cannot permit it. We have not allowed it. Today, a killer without a conscience, a man who not only admits his crimes but boasts openly of them, is in custody. While we cannot praise enough the efforts of the entire team of dedicated detectives—truly New York's Finest—who tracked him down, it was Lieutenant Marten's painstaking and inspired analysis of this multiple murderer's habits that led to his apprehension." (Here the Commissioner was paraphrasing the *New York Times*. The *Daily News* caption under Balthazar's photo referred to him as the "super sleuth who cornered the rabid Rat.")

Balthazar's pleasure had been so real that he ignored the upholstered rhetoric, the media show. He'd smiled past the glare of the lights, the thicket of microphones into the crowd where his wife was sitting, sure that she was smiling, too.

The second time Balthazar met the Commissioner was six months later at the memorial service.

On this third occasion, the Commissioner was sitting behind his elegant rosewood desk, wearing an elegant gray suit. In a beautifully modulated voice, he expressed pleasure at seeing Balthazar again, praised his "distinguished record on the Homicide Force," spoke familiarly of his work on the River Rat case. He then explained that Balthazar had been chosen for this "lend-lease assignment" (here he'd chuckled) because, although "there are many excellent, excellent officers now on the New York police force who have themselves been born in Puerto Rico," none had Balthazar's particular background and expertise. He had made several remarks about the necessity of good rapport between sister police departments, pointing out the number of times the Puerto Rican Police had helped "us and our good citizens in the past."

And, of course, Balthazar's fluent Spanish would make him doubly useful since he would be a "splendid ambassador for the New York Police." He had stood smiling by the door to his penthouse office, clasped Balthazar's hand warmly, and assured him he "envied you your stay in the Caribbean in January."

Nor had Mike Helmsley, riding back with him to the precinct, been at all helpful. Worse, Mike had been hearty. Balthazar had instantly become suspicious.

Helmsley's explanations had made it all seem very reasonable.

Point One: (Helmsley had ticked them off on his thick fingers.) The Puerto Rican brass and the DEA boys wanted the casino given a quiet once-over without the casino owners getting excited. After all, they looked like straight, solid American businessmen. But it was such an *ideal* laundry for drug money. There were those American banks all over Puerto Rico, there was no customs search, the island was so close to Miami and its drug-distribution systems.

Point Two: The investigation had to be conducted by someone who knew what he was doing, someone who was familiar with typical Mafia operations. Helmsley had tapped Balthazar's knee significantly.

Point Three: But it had to be done by someone who was not known to have this background, nobody now on Fraud or Vice. It should be done by a policeman, say like Homicide Lieutenant Balthazar Marten, who, because of his sterling work on the well-publicized River Rat case, was known to be a homicide detective. Everybody would surely believe that such a man could only be there in Puerto Rico working on a New York murder case.

Balthazar had stared gloomily out of the car window at the ice-covered streets when Helmsley had added, "Not only do you speak Spanish, you got that kind of skin. So what your grandparents were Dutch and Irish or something, you look kinda like a really tall Puerto Rican. And you get along with people. You always just sit there quiet and people tell you the damndest things. And you remember it all."

Helmsley had ticked his little finger. "There's only one other thing." It was for this one other thing that Balthazar had been waiting. He knew that beneath Helmsley's usually crumpled shirt beat a heart full of guile. This, whatever it turned out to be, was going to be a large problem. The Captain shifted his bulk so he could look at Balthazar squarely. "The problem is that the Puerto Rican police been gettin' all this shitty press lately. You been reading about it. They say the cops there aren't just robbers, but hired killers, too."

Here Helmsley had assumed his most sincere expression. "You know, Zar, what happens then. You were on the force when we had our problems. In Denver it took ten years of rebuilding *and* a big public relations number. People have to *trust* the police. Remember how low our morale got? It's hard on the Puerto Rican police because they always had a great record.

"So now they're walkin' real, real careful. They're not only lookin' over their shoulders to see what's gainin' on 'em, they're looking way ahead to see what just whizzed by. So this is the thing. You gotta go undercover, but you can't even tell the San Juan guys that what you're doin' is checking out the new casino. What the hell's the name? Yeah. The Palms. *Now* that's hard, not bein' up front, what with them so nervous already. They gotta be afraid there's a Serpico under every . . . what the hell they call those embroidered shirts the detectives wear down there?"

"Guayaberas," Balthazar had answered shortly. There was no way out of this. None. He'd stared at his hands. On this assignment, he'd be working alone, and he liked working with a partner. He thought better out loud. And while it was an important job and one that called for some expertise, which he had, the narcs had sharp-eyed accountants who could do it as well. Or better. All they needed from him was his name. Balthazar Marten, Semi-Famous Homicide Detective.

It was a comfortable stakeout. Air-conditioned casino. Probably good food. Any number of the other men would jump at it. Take the boredom involved if sunshine came with it. But he'd been doing mind-rotting paperwork for almost a year now, dragging his useless leg around headquarters. A first-class secretary could have done twice the work at half his salary. He was, he thought bitterly, a really expendable member of the Homicide Department.

But then what difference did it make? For a year he hadn't been able to care, to move, to feel.

As a child, he'd seen a display at the Museum of Natural History of a model of a caveman, supposedly frozen in ice. Holding a club, about to take a wary step forward, the man's figure was arrested as if the Ice Age had descended without a second's warning. He himself was a man encased in transparent ice.

"Yeah, well, it's hot down there, I guess, even in the winter." Helmsley was still talking. "Anyhow, you ain't there to check on the Puerto Rican cops. That *ain't* New York's problem. But you know if they think you're any kind of undercover, they're gonna think you're watchin' them. But you ain't."

He'd emphasized his point by lightly striking Balthazar's knee again. "Geez, Zar, that's not your bad knee, is it? Good, well, the reason you can't tell them what you're doin' is that you gotta know with all that loose change floatin' around from gambling that there's some cop on every casino owner's payroll. Owners just want to know what's comin' down, even if it's nothin' to do with them. But none of the owners, even the ones we're not worrying about, can hear that you're checkin' out the new place or *everybody'll* know.

"So here only I know what you're doin'—and the Commissioner. There he's okay—he never even lets his right hand know that the left just wiped his ass. In San Juan their Superintendent knows and so does a captain named Almon. Ran a good check on him. Nobody else. Best we could do. Like they say, three guys can keep a secret if two of them are already dead."

Helmsley'd nodded judiciously. "It'll work. You got your name in the papers on the River Rat case. Everybody knows you're *Homicide*.

"One more thing I gotta say. For an experienced officer, you still think you gotta do it all, Zar. You're not there to solve all the crime on the island. Just check out the damned casino. Then you go stretch out in the sun a lot, rest your leg."

Now, waiting for takeoff, Balthazar uncomfortably shifted in his seat, trying to ease the pain in his knee. There was the nagging ache; worse, the constant reminder. Rose. She had been sitting in the sunlit breakfast room of their brownstone, hunched over the crossword puzzle. She'd been dressed in blue jeans and her favorite sweater, which was actually his. A big white cable-knit Irish wool. She had looked up and said, "Oh, Zar, you'll be late. And the car might not start. Go—finish dressing."

And he had hurried up the stairs, down the stairs, out the door, and saw her now in his ski cap and old blue parka at the wheel, the snow brushed off the car, her face scrunched in concentration. She hated cold, was happy that her work could be done at home in the winter. But this time she had hurried out in the January morning to help him. She saw him coming, turned to smile, turned the ignition switch.

The car had disintegrated in a roar of heat and light; he only remembered falling, falling in the snow as the sharp metal pierced his body. When he awakened, full of pain, his leg was in a cast, the blood seeping through the white plaster, around the knee, in the shape of a rose. Rose red. Rose dead.

They had operated three times, picking out the pieces of metal. The last time he had overcome his apathy long enough to dream of not awakening, of staying down in the quiet dark, had even seen Rose smiling over her shoulder again, just ahead.

But someone held his arm, was insistent enough so that he had to open his eyes one more time, just long enough to say, "Let go." It was MacAtee, and by the time he had focused his eyes, his friend was sitting in the bedside chair, looking intrigued. MacAtee was, Rose had said, an off-the-rack Gary Cooper: same long skull, bony face, pale, no-color eyes. But T.'s eyes never had the look of someone staring somberly at distant mountains; he had a skeptical, sidelong look and a receding hairline. His oldest friend, since high school, even though MacAtee was now a successful bookie.

"Hey, Balls, you awake? That fat sergeant from the Seventh wanted to fire a dime on your ass, but I couldn't lay it off."

"Should have held it yourself, T.," he muttered, refusing to move.

"I'd lose. You'll live. I know you, Balls. So maybe the big Mafia boys themselves got those guys that did your car. After all, the mob don't want any part of that kind of trouble with the cops. They must have decided Louie just got *too* crazy. But they're out there—the BGs—bad guys. And you want to get 'em. Right, Balls? So why else you kept begging to get outta Vice and on Homicide? There it's easier to pick out the BGs. Your heart's in the right place—left of the sternum." MacAtee's laugh was always somewhere between a cackle and a snort, Balthazar thought as he drifted back into a gray darkness.

During the intervening months, Balthazar had not felt alive. He had moved from the hospital to an apartment in Manhattan. He never returned to the brownstone in Brooklyn. He went from his desk in the precinct office to the apartment and back to his desk. Now he had been given barely enough time to pack and call MacAtee and say he was off to Puerto Rico.

"Ho, ho, Balls. PR, huh? You always said you didn't like the PRs and now you'll have a whole island full of 'em. Nice island, though. Warm sun. Miles of white beaches. *Not* crowded. See, it's seventy-five degrees, but it's *winter*. PRs don't swim in the winter. But they smile, 'You wish to swim, Señor? In the *ocean*? I bring you a towel.' Hell, the dealers in the casino even smile. Except when you lose— then they feel bad. I swear to God. Hell, in Atlantic City, you win two bucks, even the pit boss looks mad.

"But, Balls, the *turistas* swim. Little snowbirds fleeing to the warm sunshine, wearing little bikinis. *Amazing* tits. Take your mirror sunglasses. And *turistas* from South America. In string bikinis. Ever see a string bikini?" MacAtee paused reverently. "I'll be there myself per usual right after the Super Bowl. Gotta pay off my P's and then I'll head down. Some of the players that owe *me* will take a little finding, but I'll see you on the beach."

Hurling now down the runway, the 747 soared upward as if it were light and the surrounding air heavy. Below him, the receding city looked to Balthazar like a black and white photograph. Then it disappeared, little by little, into the mist and snow.

He loosened his tie, took off the tan linen sportcoat he'd shivered in all the way to the airport, folded it in the empty seat next to him. He took out the novel set in the Caribbean that he'd picked up at the airport, thinking it would make good beach reading. But his eyes wouldn't focus; all night his knee had throbbed and he'd had little sleep.

An avuncular steward, a Puerto Rican in his early forties, came down the aisle distributing small, plump pillows. Taking one, Balthazar tucked it against the wall next to the window. Leaning over, the steward asked cheerfully, "Shall I wake you for breakfast, sir?"

"No, no, I don't think so," Balthazar mumbled, closing his eyes. He dozed off before the movie started.

The bump at landing, although gentle, jarred him awake. Blinking at the sun's bright dazzle outside his window, he saw dark green summer mountains against a perfect, tropical blue sky. On the movie screen ahead of him, a shot of the pilot and co-pilot at their controls appeared. The passengers applauded loudly. He couldn't remember before hearing people clap when they landed.

2

BALTHAZAR WALKED STIFFLY down the crowded concourse at Luis Muñoz Marin Airport in San Juan. The terminal was light, bright, well designed, and he realized with a grimace that he was, somehow, not expecting that. His long assignment as a young detective in New York's Spanish Harlem had soured him on Puerto Ricans. His Aunt Gretje, who had raised him, had instilled in him her Dutch passion for ordered life, for tidiness. And in that ghetto he had found too much crowding, too much litter, dirt, despair, too many vacant-eyed drug addicts. Even, he had to admit to himself, too much Latin exuberance, spontaneity. He distrusted the intense desire to live for the day.

Yet it was odd, too, because his first partner, Jorge Garrido, had been a Puerto Rican, and the best. The older man had taught him a thousand survival tricks. He had unobtrusively corrected the college Spanish Balthazar was so proud of, had enlivened their long stakeouts with stories of his countless aunts, uncles, cousins and their undying interest in different ways to roast a pig, barbecue a chicken, make a good sauce. At the time Balthazar had wondered if Puerto Ricans became bus boys because that was the most common job opening or because they were all fascinated by cooking. Jorge's own street smarts had not saved him when. . . .

He found himself in the baggage claim area. It bordered on a small courtyard, full of sunshine, green leaves, and enormous red hibiscus. The air coming through the open windows, though still smelling vaguely of airplane fuel, was soft and light. The change from the sharp, gray cold that he had left behind at Kennedy was so abrupt that he rolled up his sleeves and stared. A buxom woman checking the luggage tags of the passengers caught his eye and smiled as if she understood. He picked up his bags and went in search of a phone.

He identified himself to the policewoman who answered, and asked for Captain Almon. There was a rather long pause and then he was politely asked to hold.

At last, a young man's voice in accented English. "This is Agente Sixto Cardenas, Lieutenant Marten. We were, of course, expecting you. Of course, arrangements have been made. But you will understand that with the finding of the second body last night we are . . . mmm . . . somewhat . . . mmm . . . deranged. I myself will meet you. If you will go outside . . . you came on American Airlines? Go to the taxi stand and wait. I will be there soon." He hung up.

Balthazar stared at the phone for a long moment. Body?

Perhaps he'd misunderstood the young officer's English. He had been speaking quickly and was clearly excited. Balthazar turned to the newspaper kiosks. The *San Juan Star* headlined SECOND GIRL FOUND STRANGLED and the several Spanish language papers, one in bright red type, proclaimed SEX KILLER STRIKES AGAIN and STUDENTS PREY TO SEX FIEND.

As he drove hurriedly to the airport, Agente Sixto Cardenas worried about several things at once. He regretted that he was wearing an old *guayabera* and besides it was badly wrinkled because he had not been home for twenty-four hours. His mother would not let him leave home with even an unpressed handkerchief. The Lieutenant would think. . . . No, such an experienced man would understand, since he himself would doubtless have often been involved in such situations.

In the normal course of events, the young detective would never have been assigned to meet the lieutenant. Indeed he had not even been assigned. Herman Villareal, the Chief of Homicide One, had looked up tiredly on hearing his information and said shortly, "The Captain is not to be disturbed. You take care of it." As Sixto turned to go, Villareal had added, "Take him a gun. Make him feel at home." Sixto had paused. Surely that could wait. Perhaps the Chief was joking. But no, at the best of times, Villareal never even smiled. Sixto had gone to get a gun and boot holster from the Armory in the basement before leaving.

Sixto had known of Marten's coming and had been impressed. Only last January, when Sixto was visiting his aunt and uncle in New York he had read all the stories in the papers. When the car had been blown up (doubtless because the Lieutenant was himself a terrifying threat to the Mafia, doubtless because he could never be bribed), the press had also carried an account of Balthazar Marten's part in the successful conclusion of the River Rat case, where the man had stabbed nine prostitutes, one after another, and thrown them into the East—

Sixto smote the steering wheel in despair. Of course he would be expected to give a coherent account of their own murder case. But he'd had time to read only a few of the reports, now rapidly piling up in the room set aside for the investigation of the killer, whom the press unimaginatively—but ominously, given previous American cases—had dubbed the Student Strangler.

But, of course, the Lieutenant had come on another assignment surely, since they had known of his impending arrival days ago. Still, he would be most interested in such a case and if he, Sixto, could not even give important details, the San Juan police force would seem unprofessional, disorganized. True, they had never had a serial murderer before.

Crimes of passion, yes, constantly. The Puerto Rican preoccupation with sex caused a lot of trouble, Sixto thought, with a great deal of sympathy. And it frequently led to murder. But the Strangler was different. Still, one must give a fellow officer the impression that the investigation is solidly in hand.

The Lieutenant would be in need of lunch. Perhaps it would be possible to plead the pressure of the case and drop him at his hotel. Thank heavens, Constanzia, the only woman detective, efficient as always, had known of the arrangements. No, no, that would seem rude. Besides, this would be the only chance Sixto would have to talk to him. The man was an expert; he could learn from him. And when he finally got home he could tell his mother about his lunch with a famous New York detective, get her mind off her fears about this murderer.

Señora Cardenas had called and called headquarters that morning, she had told him. Luckily she had only gotten through once. "Sixto," she'd wailed, "my only son and you cannot come home at night and protect your widowed mother. Your mother who lives but two small miles from the University, where this strangling monster is stalking the streets killing women! Poor cousin Ida is with me, terrified. I told her it was not safe for her to be alone, she should stay with me. But what good is that? Two old women. What could we do if he were to tear off the wrought iron on the windows and come charging in? The emergency line is doubtless as busy as yours. You would finally come home but what good would that be? I would be dead.

"Cousin Ida and I are doing all that we can. We have placed lighted votive candles all around the rooms. We pray to the saints. We leave only to rush to the store or get the newspaper. We turn the television news down low during the day so that he will not know we are here. But what are we to do at night? He will see the candles and the lights, and we cannot sit here by ourselves in the dark."

Sixto had listened patiently. She was genuinely frightened. He had asked one of his friends in the uniformed branch to stop by. She'd give him a good lunch and—Where was he going to take the Lieutenant to lunch? He could take him to . . . well, it should perhaps be a place where the hamburgers were quite good, and the seafood also. El Patio de Sam in Old San Juan. A friend of his from New York always liked that. But that would be a bit of a drive, and the narrow old streets were terribly congested at this time of day.

Still, Sixto brightened, *then* he could comment on the various sights, point to the fortress of El Morro with its sweeping view of the Atlantic, the ancient houses, the City Wall, and keep the conversation safely off the murders. Yes, and the New York newspapers had carried pictures of the Lieutenant. An older man, Sixto considered, perhaps even thirty-five, but good-looking. Tall, dark, (Sixto had wondered if he were Hispanic) with a squarish jaw. Sixto paused. Tall, dark . . . only last week, the Tarot reader had remarked on the overwhelming presence in the cards of the dark stranger and had predicted that this meeting would be an important juncture in Sixto's life.

Balthazar looked around the restaurant appreciatively. It was an airy, enclosed patio with skylights, ceiling fans, and spiky tropical plants. He took another sip of the dark, aged rum with lime and soda that the detective had recommended. It was slightly sweeter and smoother even than MacAtee's favorite bourbon. He had tried to decline the offer of lunch, knowing the pressures at the beginning of a case, but the young Puerto Rican had insisted. Probably in need of a good meal himself by now, Balthazar had thought.

And the drive here had been entirely pleasant. The clarity of the light, the pristine blue of the wide sky, brought back the freshness of boyhood summers. The long curve of the Condado with its towering hotels along white sand beaches, the tourists and their towels scattered like bright mosaic tiles, reminded him of Miami. Old San Juan with its little squares and old churches looked like pictures he had seen of New Orleans. Yet the city had a style of its own. The architecture was Spanish in influence, but the lines of many of the buildings seemed almost Scandinavian in their clean facades, free of ornamentation. The modern houses on the way in from the airport were white, trimmed in bright pastel tones with splashes of flowers in small front gardens. The elegant buildings in Old San Juan were painted in pale shades—lemon, peach, gray, green, beige, or blue with white molding and curving wrought-iron balconies.

And the young officer had proved an ideal driver, pointing out the sights yet keeping his eyes firmly fixed on the traffic. The traffic reminded him of Manhattan. Although there seemed to be few large American cars, the smaller ones filled every available inch of the road, darting enterprisingly around each other in any direction, if at all possible. But the drivers waved each other in with good humor, and while there was an occasional angry honk, most of the noise came from the bugle horns, which the drivers played with élan, much like the trumpets they resembled. If the motorists saw something that pleased them or that they objected to strongly, they let off their car burglar alarms for a brief, startling moment.

Lunch was superb. The buttery red snapper was lightly broiled; the moist fried plantains had a delicate banana taste, unlike the dry flavorless ones he had tried in New York. The coffee was the best he had ever had. He began to think he was on vacation.

The thin young man across from him did not look at all relaxed. During lunch, he'd been animated, continually brushing his thick black hair back from his forehead, gesturing with arcing, enthusiastic sweeps as he talked about San Juan. He'd given Balthazar a real sense of the city and some useful background information. He'd listened with intense interest to Balthazar's accounts of his early training in New York with Jorge, his Puerto Rican partner. Perhaps, Balthazar thought, now he would be more comfortable talking about the case that was surely on his mind. A pity—such a conversation might spoil his own feeling of content. Thank

God, it was not his problem; he had merely scanned the newspaper accounts. Still, the Puerto Rican detective deserved a return for his courtesy.

"Tell me, then, about the sex murderer."

"The man *himself*?" Sixto swallowed. "I haven't . . . as yet, we don't even . . . the pathologist's report on the second girl isn't. . . ." Sixto finally blurted out, "I don't think . . . he's not a sex killer."

Balthazar went over the sentence several times in his mind, trying to decipher the meaning. "You don't think he's a sex killer. You have information not given to the papers?"

"Oh, no . . . no. That is my idea only . . . I don't know that Headquarters would. . . ." Sixto paused miserably. Why had he said that? The rum. How could he admit that it was an intuition? After the many times Homicide Chief Villareal had impressed on him the necessity of relying on facts.

"Tell me why you have that feeling."

Sixto hesitated, looking carefully at Marten. The Lieutenant had a light crescent scar above the curve of his left eyebrow, giving the unsettling impression that he didn't trust what was being said. But he found no hint of criticism in the man's voice, nor in his steady gaze.

"I was with Chief Villareal, at the baseball field where the second girl was found. Her body was untouched—naked, but not . . . touched. The first girl was not raped or sexually molested, either. There was no sign of a struggle. The method of strangling was so efficient. I felt she did not suspect, and the killer seemed not to care."

"A man with a list," Balthazar mused. "Pick up dry cleaning, buy milk, kill young woman."

Sixto looked quickly down at his coffee.

"No, please, I'm not questioning your impression. You have to be sensitive to atmosphere. There is a great deal of support for what you say, you know." Balthazar leaned forward. "I worked on the River Rat case two years ago in New York. It went on so long. I read everything. The FBI had just started their VICAP program, had come up with their profiles of serial murderers. They found that if the man is a sexual sadist, for example, he often leaves a signature on the body. Multiple stab wounds, mutilation of the genitals—in one case, teethmarks on the victim's buttocks."

Balthazar shook his head. "But, if your killings are the work of a serial murderer, the case is unlikely to be solved very fast. You remember the Zodiac killer in San Francisco—thirty-seven murders, or so he claimed—the guy was never caught. Still, good police work can make a difference—the Son of Sam was caught through a parking ticket. You must have quite a few detectives assigned to this, given the nature of the case."

"All of us in Homicide One, Lieutenant. That has not happened before."

"All of Homicide *One*? There are two homicide squads?"

"*Sí*," Sixto grinned. "We have a lot of business."

"So do we. Who decides which squad gets which business?"

"Homicide One is given the cases which require investigation to find the murderer. Homicide Two, well, they deal with those caught with a smoking gun in hand, you know?"

"Well," Balthazar said, rising from the table reluctantly, "I should let you get back to work. I hope you have some luck on this case. The FBI says that these murderers tend to be better educated—and smarter—than most. Maybe this one will turn out to be a publicity freak and get in touch with the police. That may help."

Balthazar awoke before dawn. Late that previous afternoon, he had had a long swim in the ocean, then sat on his balcony at the Dupont Plaza overlooking the Atlantic. He had sipped a rum, staring at the light turquoise water near the beach, remembering the warmth of the welcome of the registration clerk who had thought him just another tourist, and the wide-eyed smile of the small boy in the lobby who had spied the gun strapped to his boot and knew better. A handsome child. A congenial island. And he'd mulled over the question of the casino investigation. He'd begin first thing in the morning.

He'd felt agreeably detached from life, instead of isolated from it. Swimming was now the only possible exercise for him, and his body, once so used to regular workouts, had ached for vigorous movement. The warm salt water had massaged him like a giant Jacuzzi and he had been sleepy. Meaning to lie down for a brief nap, he had slid into a dreamless sleep that had lasted all night.

Another swim now, he thought, arching his back, a hot breakfast, more of that good coffee. He needn't even come back to his room. Take a robe, clean off the sand in the outside shower by the pool, and stroll into the tiled downstairs Terrace Café.

As he started his second cup of coffee, Balthazar reached idly for the discarded newspaper left on the next table. STRANGLER STRIKES A THIRD TIME!!!!! Whatever else he is, Balthazar thought, the man *is* efficient. Three murders in as many days. It seemed the work of one man; imitators would not appear this quickly. And, in any case, he noted the police had not released the method of strangulation. The girls had apparently all been killed in the same way. All were naked, all were connected with the university. Interestingly, all were athletes: a swimmer, a baseball player, an aerobics instructor.

On the second page, a bylined story by one of the many journalists keeping a vigil gave an account of a pre-dawn conference by the Secretary of Justice.

Although Secretary Cortes had only moments before received the report of the finding of the body of Imelda Torres and was not able to provide any information other than that she had been strangled, he did announce one new development. "At present, the Federal Bureau of Investigation is only keeping a watching brief. However, we ourselves have called in a noted expert in serial murder investigations. Yesterday Lieutenant Balthazar Marten of the New York Police Force. . . ."

Balthazar almost choked on the excellent coffee.

3

SAN JUAN POLICE Headquarters towers above the sprawling shopping mall, the Plaza Las Americas, to the east. From a distance, the building resembles a modern high rise office block, although one unusually burdened with antennas. But the windows are like the slits of a fortress, and the elegant base of travertine marble slants inward, a reminder of the fortified old city walls.

Now it looked like a building under siege. Sweating traffic patrolmen, despite their constant whistling and waving, could only keep the packed cars moving at a funeral cortege pace down the broad Avenida de Franklin Delano Roosevelt in front of the building and on the narrow side street between an enormous U.S. Post Office and the police parking lot behind headquarters. A post office employee frantically shooed the vehicles of the press and curiosity seekers out of that building's lot in order to let in postal patrons. But bystanders covered the median between the two, zigzagging in and out of traffic, slowing the cars of both the police and the stamp buyers. Across the Avenida, television stations and the larger newspapers had set up temporary command posts in vans in the parking lot of the Roberto Clemente Coliseum so that they could rush across the street at any sign of a possible interview. People gathered to stare at both the press and the *Policía*. Sidewalk vendors gathered to sell food to the people—crunchy pork rinds, hot dogs, and sweet cane sugar in small paper cups.

Inside, on the tenth floor, Balthazar was just shaking hands with an obviously embarrassed, and clearly exhausted, Captain Almon. Looking at him, Balthazar remembered Mike Helmsley after a few days on an intense murder case: his hunched shoulders, his rumpled, ink-stained shirt. No one in New York could ever figure out how he got ink stains from a ball-point pen. If Helmsley had been impressed with Almon's immaculate record, he'd be amazed at his impeccable appearance, Balthazar thought. The captain had an erect carriage, a fresh shave, and a formidably clean, pressed shirt. Only his hollow eyes betrayed the recent pressure he had been under.

"I do apologize, Lieutenant Marten, for . . . the lack of discussion regarding your new assignment. We managed to reach your Captain Helmsley very early this morning, but after he graciously allowed us to . . . er . . . recruit you, we were unable to reach you at your hotel."

The captain cleared his throat. "We have an unusual situation here. You see, the Justice Department in Puerto Rico has nothing to do with police cases. And it was the Secretary of Justice who announced the news of your . . . assignment. The duty of the Justice Department is to ferret out government corruption. We in the police force of course wish to have good relations with this department."

He spread his hands out, palms upward, and shrugged. "Now, this case has naturally attracted a great deal of attention from the media, as you undoubtedly saw. The press is camping on our doorstep. But our *Superintendente* does not feel that constant press conferences are in order. In the past, he has even tended to avoid them . . . whereas the Secretary of Justice feels that the media should be fully informed. He has been in politics here for some time. He knows many of the people in the media. And we are not unhappy that the reporters also sit outside *his* office."

He paused, looking over Balthazar's shoulder. "But the Secretary of Justice becomes upset if all he has to announce is the finding of yet another body. The public is already panicked. He wishes to report progress on the case. But in only three days, what progress can there be? When he learned that you had been sent here, although in an entirely different capacity, well . . . you see? And," he concluded unhappily, "he wishes you to report to him personally."

Almon headed for his office door. "I have made arrangements for Chief Villareal and one of his senior men, who have been on the Strangler case from the beginning, to brief you around lunch time. You will want to look at the reports first."

He stopped and turned toward Balthazar. His posture was as straight as that of the most eager young military recruit. "I'm sorry that we must put off your investigation of the Palms. But we do welcome your help with these murders. I only hope they can be solved." He paused. "Solved quickly, that is."

He opened his office door. "Also, I will assign you a driver. Perhaps you would like Agente Cardenas, whom you met yesterday. It was lucky that I saw him before he went off duty last evening." The captain's face was impassive. "When I inquired about your arrival, he told me of your abilities. He is certainly an admirer of yours."

"An *Americano*."

Balthazar, sitting in the empty Investigation Room on the second floor at Police Headquarters and engrossed in the reports, looked up, startled. The man before him had a deep white scar running from the edge of his eye to his chin. The scar was barely disguised by a close-trimmed beard. He was a tall, powerful man in his early forties. There were pouches under the dark, blank eyes fixed on Balthazar.

"Yes, I'm from New York," Balthazar replied in Spanish.

"I know. I meant the killer was an *Americano*."

"Why do you say that?"

"I *assume*." Turning his back on Balthazar, he walked stiffly down the long windowless room, jerkily rearranging the pile of papers on the table. He wheeled around. "It is an un–Puerto-Rican crime. Requires planning. We Puerto Ricans, you know, decide to do something one moment, and something else the next."

Balthazar said nothing.

"My name is Angel Negrón. In your military, they called me *An-gel*." He hit the soft *g* sound with emphasis. "They could not say *An-hell*. And they pronounced my friend's name Jesus, instead of *Hay-su*. They said *we* were too stupid to learn English." His own English was correct and unaccented.

Balthazar continued looking at the report he was holding. He thought of MacAtee's expression in situations like this: DN. Don't Need.

"And," Negrón continued, "they say we don't speak Spanish, either. They call it Spanglish. We drive *carros*, not *coches*. You learned your Spanish in college, no doubt."

"Puerto Rican partner," Balthazar said shortly.

"Ah, of course. Of course. You are sent here to solve this case for us. In New York, they sent you with him to take care of him."

"He's dead," Balthazar said.

After Negrón left, Balthazar tried to push aside the feeling of intense dislike that the man's hostility had aroused in him, but he could not. Was Negrón's resentment a reflex stemming from his past experience with Anglos? A reflection perhaps of what Jorge had only half-jokingly called "the Puerto Rican national inferiority complex"? Or was it primarily a territorial number? Would the rest of the detectives be this antagonistic? Under other circumstances, he could imagine quite a few would be. He was familiar enough with the stories that Helmsley had been referring to on the problems of the *Policía*. The Teresa Casera scandal had been given a big play in the *Daily News* and headlined in the New York Spanish-language papers. Not more than two months ago—everybody's skin would still be raw; everybody suspicious of an interloper.

But in this case, given the urgency to find the killer and find him immediately, a trained extra man should be seen as useful. In the damned River Rat case, the New York force had even welcomed the FBI.

Negrón's animosity seemed almost personal. . . . Balthazar determinedly picked up the reports in front of him again. But, as he read, Negrón's phrase on the "un–Puerto-Rican" nature of the crimes stayed in his mind. There was something unusual, at least, about the pattern of these murders that disturbed him as well. What was it?

It was clear that a great deal of organization was required. Negrón was right. Few murder cases show any sign of organization. People lead messy lives; their murders are messy, too. This killer had been very careful. The only sign of his presence had been the scrapings under the first two victims' nails. And that had been mystifying—not helpful.

It was always unusual when a man killed strangers. People he didn't know. Puerto Ricans *were* much more likely to kill family members, friends, or lovers. But so were all other Americans—black, white, or Hispanic. So were the French, the Italians. Swedes, well, they tended to kill themselves. That line of thinking led nowhere.

What else? The time frame. Three murders in three days. Very uncommon. Fast, and professional. The man knew a great deal about murder.

The young Puerto Rican agent, Sixto Cardenas, had said that what struck him about the murders was their lack of passion. Yes, Balthazar thought, sitting up, the killer seemed detached, but he *strangled* his victims. Those two elements didn't fit the patterns that showed up in the FBI studies. He had pored over their findings when he worked on the River Rat case. He remembered the statistics clearly. Granted that there were exceptions to any pattern of human behavior, especially ones that were so bizarre to begin with. Still, it was a place to start.

The FBI had found that men—and they were always men—who killed strangers belonged generally to two very different groups who killed in two very different ways. In one category there were those who heard voices, voices no one else heard. They often had original ideas about life in the next world or very peculiar explanations about life here. They were aggressive men, suspicious, hostile. That made them dangerous.

There was, for example, John Linley Frazier. He had shot an eye surgeon he'd never met—and the doctor's entire family—and tossed their bodies, neatly blindfolded, into the swimming pool of their elegant hilltop mansion.

Houses like theirs clearly destroyed the fragile mountain environment, Frazier believed. He left a note pointing that out. A note full of misspellings and zeal.

He had written, "today world war 3 will begin as brought to you by the pepole of the free universe. From this day forward any one and ?/or company of persons who missuses the natural environment or destroys same will suffer the penalty of death by the people of the free universe." He had signed the note with the names of the Tarot deck of cards.

Herbert Mullin belonged to the same category. He had shot thirteen people. His purpose in killing was different. And his spelling was much better.

Mullin was solving a problem. California was scheduled for earthquakes. Earthquakes could be prevented by killing people. It had to be done, he explained to the jury. If a few people were killed, it would save millions of lives. He had been selected to do the killing because he was born on the same day that Einstein died.

These were men with twisted logic, but with missions. Psychiatrists called them paranoid schizophrenics. They did not mutilate their victims' bodies, nor did they touch them when they killed them.

The men in the second category always did that. They were the sexual sadists. Killing made them feel good—orgasmic. They almost always strangled their victims. The corpses showed signs of the killer. There was usually a length of time between their killings. As if the killer had to build up to another orgasm.

Occasionally, they sent notes. The Boston Strangler taunted the police for months. The Hillside Strangler never put pen to paper. Neither did the River Rat.

But the corpses of their strangled victims showed signs of rape or mutilation.

This killer strangled, yet left no marks. And he acted very, very quickly.

Balthazar grimaced. At first glance it did not look as if the FBI's VICAP data base. . . . Still, a few characteristics applied and one could deduce several things about the murderer. He had to begin by considering the choice of victim, the method used, and see what patterns emerged.

He began an abbreviated list of the victims:

Susan McKinley, student, swimmer, white female, 22, 5'9", 160 lbs., body found on edge of San Juan Bay by traffic patrolman. Time of death: approximately 8:30 P.M. Saturday, January 13.

Karen Hoover, student, baseball player, white female, 20, 5'6", 120 lbs., body found in back of university baseball stadium by janitor on his way home. Time of death: 10:30 P.M. Sunday, January 14.

Imelda Torres, file clerk and aerobics instructor, black female, 24, 5'4", estimated weight 110 lbs., body found by surveying crew in remote area near bridge construction Monday afternoon, January 15. Yesterday. Pathologist's report not complete. But she had been strangled in the same way as the other two girls.

He studied the photographs of the first girl's body and the surrounding area. She lay spread out, head turned to the side, as if she were sunbathing on that dark beach. A marathon swimmer, she was a good-sized girl, muscular, healthy. Susan McKinley's parents lived in California.

Under the police photographs was a studio portrait of the living girl, collected from a friend or relative. Her straight blonde hair came to just below her ears like a shining cap. Not beautiful, but wholesome. Blue eyes, straight nose, perfect teeth, a strong jaw. But what arrested him was her expression. She was smiling at the camera as if at a trusted friend, openly, unselfconsciously.

Bile rose in his throat, shocking him. He had almost forgotten that intense anger that overwhelmed him in a case where the innocent, the helpless were victimized. He sat rigidly, but he felt prickles in his fingers and toes, as if even his extremities had been asleep and now the blood was flowing back into them. The men who'd killed his wife were themselves dead before he left the hospital. His fury had had no object, and he had been so turned inward with grief that he'd felt no other emotion. Now his rage could not be repressed, didn't need to be. He almost savored it. He would get this killer.

He went through the next set of pictures. Karen Hoover was on her stomach, her head skewed at a painful angle. Her body had been concealed in the bushes behind the stadium, and the foliage had been bent back so the photographer could get a clear shot. Her slight, wiry body had not broken the lower branches, and her upper body seemed to rest on an inclined pillow, head and arms hanging down.

The other snapshots, clearly from university files, showed Karen in a baseball uniform, light brown curls escaping from a batter's helmet or a baseball cap. In one she stood with the bat cocked, her whole body concentrating on the pitch. In the second, she was leaping high in the infield, her mitt up, as if the ball was sure to come just there. Her parents had two addresses: one in Darien, Connecticut, and a condominium in Manhattan. Balthazar raised an eyebrow at the expensive address.

Unlike the other two, the pictures of Imelda Torres had been taken during the day. Her body had been dumped in a swampy area not far from the Loiza River. The lush growth surrounded her outflung arms and legs, almost covering the head with its tightly curled hair, as if she were merging with

the earth, Her flesh was torn by innumerable small pred-
ators. But not that, not even the quick camera focus, the
harsh light, could conceal the beauty of her graceful black
body. An aerobics instructor, possibly a dancer.

The portrait of Imelda Torres had been taken a few
years earlier—probably at her high school graduation. She
looked very young, her Afro largely hidden by the tasseled
graduation cap, dark eyes alight in a rounded face, dressed
in black gown with a white collar, a gold cross just showing
below it. He took a long look at her happy face.

He continued with his list. The "figure four" choke
hold had been used in each instance.

The killer had stood in back of each girl and put his
right arm around her neck. Then he locked his right hand
on his left bicep and pushed the girl's neck into the inside of
his elbow with his left hand. It was called the figure four
because the killer's two arms formed the numeral 4. It was a
modified judo hold. Modified because you only used it if
you intended to kill.

It was effective. The victim could not scratch at the
attacker's eyes because his head was safely tucked in back of
hers. In any case, almost everyone's first impulse was to
claw at the attacker's arm to loosen the frightening grip that
cut off air. *That* was not effective. The victim lost con-
sciousness quickly.

He looked at his list for a long time, occasionally checking the reports in front of him. He wrote his initial profile of
the killer:

—White male between 25 and 45, over average height.
—English speaker, at least a high school education, is
   intelligent and articulate.
—Has spent some time in Puerto Rico.
—Lives alone.
—Has a good income.
—Military background.
—Possibly homosexual or at least bisexual.
—No previous police record.

Recommendation: There are indications that the man is not

legally insane. Serious consideration should be given to a possible motive.

Balthazar read it through again. At least a start. One idea troubled him—the killer's sexual orientation. The longer he looked at the details of the case, the more firmly he shared Cardenas's intuitive assessment. These killings did not spring from any form of lust. It was the stark absence of feeling surrounding them that gripped his own imagination, made him certain there was a motive somewhere. But VICAP's statistics leaned heavily toward a non-heterosexual. He felt required to add it to his own profile, although he'd qualified it with a "possibly."

And he was also sure that the person capable of committing these murders had never been loved, and therefore could not care about others, could only view people as objects. Here there was every sign of a neglected, abused child, or one adopted by necessity. Yet he could hardly substantiate such a perception. He would find it difficult to discuss impressions with men he'd never met before, never worked with.

He stood up. If he could just think of something intelligent to say about those odd fingernail scrapings. He hoped uncomfortably that the Homicide One team was not taking the newspapers' description of him as an expert too literally.

4

"YES. YES. A VERY impressive profile of the killer, Lieutenant."

Homicide Chief Villareal nervously straightened a mustache that drooped slightly around the edges of his mouth with his index finger and thumb. He was a spare older man with intelligent, hooded eyes. He cleared his throat and slipped a small square of candy-coated gum into his mouth. "Very interesting. And in many ways similar to our own. Some differences. We must discuss these. And of course fill you in on the steps we've taken so far."

Villareal had come to the meeting in the Investigation Room looking morose. Now he looked uneasy as well, Balthazar decided, and he wondered if what he had written caused that reaction. Given the man's unconscious patting of his upper shirt pocket, perhaps it was simply that he'd quit smoking recently and sitting still was difficult. Or was it the presence of a new, and possibly unwanted, man on the team?

Balthazar looked around the table. Sixto Cardenas looked much better for a few hours sleep and a fresh shirt. His shy, friendly smile and warm handshake had been the one cordial note in the introductions.

He was seated next to the fourth man, Villareal's second in command, who had been introduced as Oscar Montez. Although not as tall as Balthazar, Montez had the build of a sumo wrestler. Even his mustache was huge. He looked enormously strong. He was certainly silent at the moment. He took a third sandwich from the lunch tray on the table and chewed slowly and thoroughly.

Villareal looked up from the sheet of notes Balthazar had handed him. "You would like to explain your reasoning, Lieutenant?"

"The murderer does not fit documented patterns for random killers, as I'm sure you know. Of course, only about seventy percent of them do."

The room was very quiet. Looking up, Balthazar saw Villareal and Montez exchanging glances. He went on hastily.

"I'm looking, obviously, at the method of killing—not characteristic of the schizophrenics at all—and the absence of sexual assault—which is very unlike the sadists."

"An unusual crazy," Villareal interjected. Montez got up, poured himself more coffee and sat down again, scraping his chair across the floor.

"Well," Balthazar hesitated, "possibly. The guy could be a schizo who has decided that the planets will stop spinning if women go to college instead of staying home and having babies and he just hasn't gotten around to telling us that yet. But those men have always used hands-off killing methods. Guns, most of the time. Much less likely to leave clues. That's why it takes so long to catch them. And while they can be very intelligent, they don't really use this much foresight. Too intent on their mission, maybe."

He waited for comment, but none of the three men spoke. Perhaps, Balthazar thought, they disagree entirely and are merely being polite to an outsider.

He went on. "Or he could be a sexual sadist who just doesn't fit the mold. Gets his sexual thrills all in his head."

Montez nodded slowly and thoughtfully.

"The point is," Balthazar said, "that I used data from previous cases for only a few of these characteristics—I see the killer as a white male because there has only been one exception. And while one of the victims was a black, two were white. Killers choose victims from their own ethnic group. I focused on what evidence we have for the rest of the profile."

He paused. "But I drew no conclusions from the victims' fingernail scrapings. One assumes these women scratched the man's arms. But instead of skin, we find. . . . Well, I didn't know what to make of the findings."

Villareal tapped a pile of papers with weary disgust. "What we have learned since makes the problem worse. Please continue."

"The figure four choke hold indicates the height and age group. A much older man is less likely to choose a method that depends so much on quickness of reflex, although this method does not necessarily require strength. A man younger than twenty-five is hardly ever as careful to erase clues as this man."

He checked his profile. "The intelligence I'm sure of. He plans, yet he is capable of seizing opportunity. The educational level I'm guessing at. Consider all that he knows. And he must be articulate. I'd guess even quite glib. He certainly must speak English well. The reports indicate that the swimmer, Susan McKinley, spoke little Spanish. Now he could have jumped Karen Hoover behind the baseball stadium, but he had to have spoken to the McKinley girl. The photos show no cover on that beach where she was killed. I don't see how he could have surprised her. I can't even imagine why she'd have been on that beach. On the map, it looks as if it's surrounded by factories. It seemed funny to me that—"

"*Sí*," Sixto cut in. "We have much better beaches, but the Bay is often used for marathon training. The right distance, you see. One has a friend with a boat who follows alongside. We do not know why she would have been there alone, of course. Her car was left there."

Balthazar nodded. "Okay, so the killer himself must own a car. And I'd bet he lives alone—imagine his weekend activities. Those two things take some money. And given the locations of the bodies, he knows the island and is therefore not a recent arrival."

He smiled ruefully at the next item on his list. "Military background because of the chokehold. But seeing the size of the army and navy bases on this island, that probably isn't going to help us much, is it? Or the killer could have had combat training in ROTC classes at the university, too, I suppose."

"*Sí*," Villareal said. "And so many Puerto Ricans have been in one of the services—half the island. But why do you believe our killer has no police record?"

"He doesn't seem an impulsive man by nature—too calculating. If he robs, he's clever enough not to get caught. If these are not his first killings, he seems literally to be getting away with murder. And, although I don't think that computer data on earlier cases is going to help here, other random killers have not usually had a record. Not even the sexual sadists—for any kind of previous sex offenses. Gacy, the one outside of Chicago who killed thirty-three young men, was an exception. He did have a prior—for sodomy. It was in another state and wasn't noted until much later."

"Ah, there," Villareal said, looking at the ceiling, "we feel that this aspect must be checked carefully. FBI data— and we take these studies very seriously—show that killers in that latter group are homosexual, or at least bisexual. The fingernail scrapings under the victims' nails indicate that our killer was wearing very . . . peculiar clothing. So we are checking out the homosexual community."

"You have in mind especially the shreds of leather under the baseball player's nails?" Balthazar asked.

"Wash leather," Villareal answered. "Untanned, coarse, often used in heavy hunting jackets. The man could not walk about here in such a long-sleeved jacket. It would be much too warm. People would stare. He would hardly want that."

"But the small pieces of rubber under the swimmer's nails," Balthazar said. "Wet suit material?"

"It is true," Villareal said glumly, "that such material is used in making wet suits, Lieutenant. But you understand that it makes no sense, anyway. A swimmer would be much too hot in such a suit near the surface, and a deep sea diver would hardly have been coming ashore there. If the man deliberately put on such a suit to avoid scratches, the McKinley girl, an experienced swimmer, would have thought it very odd."

"The man would not have considered that. He is quite mad," Montez said firmly.

"Well," Balthazar said, choosing his words carefully, "perhaps, but if so, he can still subtract backward by sevens. That's why I came to the conclusion that he was legally sane. And even those who are certifiably crazy take care not to be caught. During the Son of Sam investigation in New York, one of our men said, 'Okay, so the killer is a loony. He still didn't hop into the subway with a goddamned big rifle.' So we started checking parking tickets in the area of the murders. I'm convinced the man has a motive."

"But a motive that would make no sense to us," Montez said slowly. "I love *beisbol*, and I have seen that girl, Karen Hoover, play. A shortstop—everywhere in the infield she caught the ball. They called her 'the Vacuum Cleaner.' A joke, no? To kill a girl so full of life. I could never understand such a man's thinking." He shook his head, and then amended his statement. "Unless of course he was her lover."

"Still, I think," Balthazar went on doggedly, "and I'm sure you'll agree, that these women's backgrounds must be thoroughly checked."

"But, of course, Lieutenant," Villareal interposed. "By all means. We are not ruling out any possibility. When the McKinley girl's body was found, we naturally began a detailed investigation of her background—fellow students with ROTC training and so forth. Our men are doing this now on Karen Hoover. As yet, we have not turned up any connection between these girls. No classes together. No common friends. But it is a large university. And we have only begun. So far we have no information on the Torres girl. We were extremely lucky to have even identified her so quickly. But we are making no assumptions about this man and—"

"It would not even have to be a man," Sixto broke in. "A woman in some ways would be more likely. A woman *pervert*," he added excitedly. "She would not need to be large or strong to use the chokehold, but all the victims were athletes, and they would know many strong women. The victims would be much less suspicious of a stranger if it were a woman and—"

"It is only more convenient to refer to the killer as a man," Villareal said tiredly, "and as the lieutenant said, in the past, such killers have always been men."

"Again," Sixto went on, "the killer could be sane and have a motive but not one that has anything to do with any of these women. I—"

Villareal gathered up his papers quickly, and to Balthazar's considerable surprise, stood up. "There are many possibilities, Cardenas," he said brusquely. "And all must be considered. At present we will assume nothing, and our routines are set up to exclude nothing. *Rutina*," he added sententiously, "will solve this case, not imaginative speculation, not *intuición*. Now, perhaps, you will see to proper identification for the lieutenant, and fill him in on those aspects we have not covered."

He motioned to Montez to follow him, and then turned to Balthazar. "We are grateful for your help. If you and Cardenas will concentrate on the organization of the reports on the girls' backgrounds, it would be very useful for us. If there is a motive, you will see it."

As they strode down the hall, Villareal muttered to Montez. "Cardenas is quick. You heard him. What if he too begins to suspect . . . ?"

"And if he does?" Montez shrugged his massive shoulders. "We will tell him that we are investigating. This is an internal matter. He will see that this must not be rumored about—the press must not hear of it. And he will see there is no need to discuss this with an outsider."

"The lieutenant will think we are keeping information from him. He is a young man, particularly for his rank. He could be impetuous—"

"I think him a reasonable man. And," Montez added dryly, "suspecting a member of one's own department is not unheard of in New York."

"It is not as if we had evidence. It is only the question of a possible motive. And," Villareal added, "the fact that these murders are so . . . professional."

"*Stranglings*," Montez underlined.

"If only Negrón had been on duty this weekend," Villareal fretted. "Then we would have certain hours accounted for. At least we would know. . . ."

"But we will find out in any case," Montez said. "Many people know Negrón."

"Have you asked *El Vampiro* what he has heard?"

"I have left a message for him," Montez replied. "In this case, he may help. He has a daughter."

5

STRANGLER WEARS LEATHER!!! The headlines in all the newspapers, both Spanish and English, were again almost identical. Young boys rushed up to the cars at every stoplight, thrusting out the latest editions of *El Reportero, El Nuevo Día,* the *San Juan Star, El Mundo, El Clamor.* Every motorist bought at least one paper. Balthazar winced and turned to Sixto, who frowned over the steering wheel.

"I suppose they *had* to release the information on the fingernail scrapings to the press. Somebody might have seen the guy at least carrying the jacket."

"*Sí.* As Chief Villareal said, much faith is put in the data that suggest the man is a homosexual. Such men," Sixto added with flat disapproval, "dress in strange ways. And they know which of them would be," he paused, searching for the right English word, "be. . . ."

"A leather freak?" Balthazar suggested. "Right, and the police will probably get more cooperation from the gays if they know there's a particular reason for their questions."

"*Sí*. The Chief said that the *patos* were complaining. They felt they were being harassed simply because they are homosexuals. For no cause." Sixto considered. "He also said that in the past, they would never have made complaints. They would not even have thought of it. Not for a single moment."

"The trouble is that these articles make the killer sound like a drooling maniac. I'm beginning to think there's a very small minority who consider the man might have a motive."

"A very small minority," Sixto agreed ruefully. "You and I."

"But look, he may not have a motive for killing that first girl, the swimmer. But he must have known her, or known somehow she'd be at that beach. He couldn't see her from the highway. How does he get her there?"

"Well," Sixto said thoughtfully, "she was a *gringo*."

"That makes her more likely to go off with a stranger?"

"Oh, no, no. I do not mean that she would then have loose morals. Not at all, Lieutenant. It is only that, you see, Puerto Rican girls who are of such a class, who go to the university . . . if a stranger were to speak to them, they would just look at him very coldly. . . . They would not reply. . . . Their mothers are very strict. . . . But I am sure that the mothers of the *norteamericano* girls are also very strict. . . . It is only that I find that if I speak to the girls from the States, they smile, whereas. . . . I myself can never think of what to say to the Puerto Rican girls, I am sure that is the problem," he concluded miserably, afraid that he had offended the Lieutenant.

"You may have a point. A cultural difference. But it would depend a great deal on the particular girl. I'll be interested in what this woman English professor, Maria Knight, has to say about Susan's personality. Apparently she was not only in one of her classes, but baby-sat for the professor's nephew as well. Let's try her home before going to the university. She lives in Río Piedras. Calle Laurel de India, number twenty-four."

Sixto raised his eyebrows. "You have a good memory."

"Photographic," Balthazar grinned. "Very helpful in college exams. And once in a while in the detective biz. But it's only good for the short term. Don't ask me for this woman's address next week."

They stopped in front of a small white house with attractive landscaping. The neighboring gardens were filled with the flamboyant red hibiscus and dark pink bougainvilleas that grew everywhere naturally, but here someone had also planted magnolia, jasmine, gardenias. Their fragrances surrounded the house, hung on the hot heavy air, and he thought nostalgically of the white gardenias his aunt had grown on their sun porch in Brooklyn.

The woman who opened the door was very attractive. The severe black dress she was wearing set off the intense whiteness of her face and arms. She was tall, with ash-blonde, sun-streaked hair pulled back in a chignon. Her light eyes were faintly red-rimmed, and she looked weary.

"My name is actually Maira Knight, not Maria," she replied to Sixto's question. Her voice had the trace of a New York accent. "M-A-*I-R*-A. But everyone gets it wrong one way or the other. Puerto Ricans spell it M-A-Y-R-A, but it's pronounced Mare-a. Would you like to come in, officers?"

The living room was airy, cool after the insistent sunlight. The blue walls were lined with white bookcases filled with books. Vases of flowers stood on the white wicker tables; the plump pillows of the matching couches looked comfortably used.

As they sat down, Balthazar, trying hard not to stare at her, found his throat was a little dry. He remarked in what he hoped was a conversational tone, "You have such fair skin. 'Mad dogs and Englishmen go out in the noon-day sun,' but never English professors?"

"Not without wearing a sun blocker." She smiled at his quote. "Or I turn an unprepossessing cooked-shrimp color. As another of my pale friends puts it, 'We only get a precancerous glow.' Of course, some blondes tan beautifully. Susan, for example. . . ." She pressed her lips together and grimaced. "The McKinleys—Susan's parents—just left.

They stayed last night at a hotel, but they're on their way now to Fajardo, to visit old friends of theirs in the military. He was stationed here before they retired to California. They're older people; Susan was their youngest, and this has been very hard on them. I'm sorry you missed them. That's why you came?"

"We wanted to talk to you about Susan, too. Was she the sort of friendly girl who would be apt to chat with strangers?"

"That depends. Susan wouldn't pick up a stranger, certainly. For one thing, she was very shy." She paused. "Well, I suppose I could imagine her talking to one at length, though. A very plausible stranger or a slight acquaintance, for example. She was very friendly. But, you see, *I* thought Susan was lovely. So fresh faced . . . and eager. But, partly because of her size . . . she always thought she was too fat— unattractive to men. But it was muscle—she lifted weights. She was very healthy, in superb condition."

She faltered a little, perhaps over the irony of the death of the young and strong. Clearing her throat, she continued. "Her attitude about her appearance might have made her a little vulnerable to some men's attentions. And she was lonely. I'm sure that's why she came here so often, even when I didn't need her to baby-sit. Of course, she was very fond of the boys, and Lena, my housekeeper, was teaching her to cook."

"You have two boys?"

"No," she replied. She had, Balthazar thought, what his aunt would have called a 'speaking face.' Despite the strain she was under, her face was animated, her smile warm and direct. Her eyes were not just light, but full of light. It was hard to concentrate on what she was saying. "My nephew Rico lives with me, as well as Lena's son, Juan, who's also five."

"She didn't have a boyfriend?" His throat seemed to be getting drier.

"Well, no, not really. Her only close male friend was John Haverford. He always followed her in his motorboat and timed her Bay swims. They shared a real enthusiasm for water sports. He has a sailboat, too, and Susan crewed for him. But they weren't . . . romantically involved. John is a brilliant boy, but a little odd, I'd say. I think he cared for Susan a great deal."

"So, if he'd suggested that they go to the Bay, even at night, she wouldn't have hesitated?"

"Well, I don't . . . but surely, Lieutenant, the papers indicate that the killer did not know the victims? I hope that my offhand remark about John is not influencing you. Let me add that I hardly meant he is mentally imbalanced. Or the sort of man who could cold-bloodedly—"

"But you see, Professor Knight," Balthazar said hastily, "we have to consider all the possibilities. You yourself said that she wouldn't simply go off with someone she didn't know."

"I also said that I could imagine circumstances," she said crisply. "For example, she was an expert Bay swimmer. If she happened to be on the beach in the afternoon and fell into conversation with someone on the subject, for example, she might have continued talking for some time, through the evening."

"The reports indicate that she was seen in her dorm room late in the afternoon. It would have been evening before she arrived at the beach. Would you mind telling us why you think of John Haverford as odd?"

"I don't think I will answer that question, Lieutenant. It is only my opinion. I like the boy very much. I know him fairly well. He came here often with Susan. He would not have killed her." She was angry.

Sixto was following the conversation intently. The Lieutenant, he thought admiringly, is not allowing himself to be swayed by the fact that the *profesora* was so very pretty, as he himself would have been. Not at all—he was questioning her closely. Very professional. People often withheld information about friends who, in their view, could not possibly be involved. And while Sixto himself would not have at first suspected her, as sad as she was about her young student, she could be an accomplished actress. She was tall and in very good shape. Amazing long legs. By arousing her anger, the Lieutenant could rattle her, even ferret out a motive if she had one.

"Did you get the impression that he was homosexual?" Balthazar regretted the words as soon as they were out of his mouth. He did not want to anger her; he should have changed the subject. He wasn't thinking clearly.

She stood up. "It seems to me that question could only be based on a well-known police prejudice against a particular group. The newspapers indicate that there seems to be no way to connect these unfortunate young women. Surely their friends and relatives do not need any additional pain, and I cannot see how it could lead to the capture of a man who kills strangers on the spur of the moment."

"Believe me, it's necessary," Balthazar replied, desperately wishing he could start over.

She remained standing, her face flushed. "There can be no justification for fishing expeditions just because you have no leads, Lieutenant."

"The killer could well be picking victims at random," Balthazar replied, stung by her remark. "But he doesn't fit the patterns of such killers in some ways. He has not gotten in touch with the police, for example, and they often do that. We're simply exploring. . . ."

A good move, Sixto thought. He releases some information not given to the public to see how she responds.

She sat down, but her voice was still chilly. "Very well, but I do not wish to be put in the position of discussing Susan's other friends. If one of us is to be a suspect, then we all are. Please confine your questions to my own actions. I'll tell you what I did this weekend."

She went on, but she refused to meet his eyes. "Saturday evening I attended the Folkloric Festival at the university. Lena took Rico and her own son to visit her parents over the weekend. At the festival, I talked with a number of my friends, including the department chairman, Carlos Santiago. I don't know when I returned, but shortly after I came home from the campus, a friend of mine dropped by. I'm sure he will vouch for my presence. Late Sunday evening, Lena returned with the boys."

"There are no other members of your household? The report lists you as Señora Knight."

"My husband is an MIA, Lieutenant. He was shot down over Vietnam six months before Saigon fell."

Balthazar rose. "I'm sorry—" he began.

The door bell chimed. He followed her, feeling agonizingly inept, to the door. On the step was a handsome marine in his early thirties, blond but with dark brown eyes and the typical rounded face of a Puerto Rican. "Paolo, this is Lieutenant Marten; Master Sergeant Paolo Davenport. The lieutenant is checking on my weekend activities. Perhaps you remember what time you came by on Saturday night?"

He nodded and looked hard at the detective. Balthazar thought he had even stiffened at first; a male's reaction to an intrusion on his territory. Well, it's only natural, he reflected, she has been all but widowed for twelve years. He himself had been married for twelve years when Rose. . . .

"Yes," Davenport said, "well, I'm not sure, but certainly before nine, I'd say."

As Balthazar followed Sixto down the walk, he heard the man remark, "You look a little upset, Maira. The boys are in the car. I'll take them to Burger King."

Balthazar glanced at the two small boys wrestling in the front seat of a Nissan, who stopped long enough to stare at the two detectives. One waved. Sixto gave them a brief salute. Balthazar felt a sharp jab of envy. Absurdly, he wanted to be the man who could help Maira Knight, comfort her, protect her. Tucking his clipboard notebook firmly under his arm, he strode down the walk, trying hard not to limp.

After a fruitless effort to locate Karen Hoover's coach, who was off at an athletic meet, Balthazar and Sixto drove toward headquarters. "Wait, let's check that Haverford kid's apartment," Balthazar suggested. "Nobody's talked to him yet. Reports indicate that he was supposed to be out sailing all weekend, but he might be back."

Haverford's apartment was in a high rise on a beach in the Condado. The security guard told them that Mr. Haverford had returned a few hours ago. "Not bad," Balthazar noted wryly, as they moved down the thickly carpeted corridor. "The sheet says the kid's unemployed."

They rang and pounded for some time before they heard a thin voice, "I'm coming, I'm coming." A young man opened the door, dressed only in a pair of shorts. Although the upper part of his scrawny body was almost hairless, he had a sparse beard and mustache, obviously grown in an effort to hide a repaired cleft palate. He stared groggily at the two men, muttering that he had been asleep. He looked carefully at their identification, however, before waving them inside. Probably trying to figure out if they were from Narcotics, Balthazar guessed.

The long living room ended in a spectacular view of the beach, now in twilight. The walls were light gray with white molding, and the room was furnished only with huge white and charcoal cushions, loosely scattered about on the floor. It looked as if a decorator had started enthusiastically, but was stopped before choosing furniture and color accents. There were two small tables cluttered with dirty glasses and piled-up books. In one corner stood an enormous Turkish hookah. Haverford sprawled on one of the pillows and leaned back with his hands laced behind his head. "So you want to ask me about old Suze? What can I tell you? I went out on the boat Friday morning, and I only got back a couple of hours ago."

He answered their questions either in monosyllables or in a sudden rush of words. His voice was high with a slight nasal honk.

"I only saw her twice since I've been back from the States. I went home for Christmas, right? To New Jersey. To *Old* Jersey. Mum always wants an old-fashioned Christmas with the whole family boring the shit out of each other. Christ. We're not even a real family. They adopted us—all of us. Sort of like buying grapefruit. Two yellows and two pinks. Two boys and two girls. Well, they have plenty of money. Oil. We were raised by the best hired help. I was bounced from four military academies."

He plucked a little nervously at his meager chest hairs. It was obvious that he did not enjoy a monologue. Uneasy about the way he sounds, Balthazar wondered, or does he just want to avoid our questions?

"So," he went on, "then we go to Miami. We always go to Miami. At least you can sail there. When I got back, Suze was studying for her exams. Couldn't sail. Miss Priss. Had to go to the library and do her little term papers. 'You've got to find something to do with your life, John. Go back to school. Finish your degree.' Sounded like my fucking parents. A lot of people spend their lives on boats. Only sensible way to live. It was a shock, though. I berth my boat in Fajardo—it can be sailed solo, better with two, though. Anyway, I rolled into the dockside café and they were all talking about the Student Strangler. I got a paper and found out. . . .

"No, I don't know what the fuck she was doing on that beach at night. I'll tell you, though, what she *wasn't* doing. She wasn't fucking. That girl always said no. I tried a couple times; she always said, 'We're friends.' Guy probably strangled her out of exasperation. Christ, what are friends for? But she was a good crew. . . .

"No, she didn't do drugs, either. In Training. Capital T. Well, pot, but only sometimes. We'd lay on the deck when the sea was calm, sunbathe, have a joint and a cold beer. Wouldn't *touch* cocaine.

"Why'd I leave on Friday? Well, officer, it was November in my soul. Just like Ishmael. Christ, even the police should know that people get on boats to get away from the land. Christ.

"What do you mean, did anyone see me? People on cruise ships, fishermen, other sailors. The Atlantic isn't empty. You think I'd go out and then whip back in and— You guys getting desperate or something?" His voice got higher, the slight snort of his repaired palate even more pronounced. "Sure, you got the papers on your ass. You have to pull in somebody. You think, 'Yeah, this Haverford, drug-crazed beach bum, he could have strangled the women.' Well, you can stuff that. You aren't pinning this on me."

He jumped up and disappeared into the bedroom and they could hear him on the phone. He returned to the living room with a sullen expression on his young face.

"Lawyer's coming down tomorrow. So, if you want a description of my fucking boat or my fucking chart, get it from him. I'm not opening my mouth again." He sat down again and crossed his arms mulishly. "You can just leave, you hear? I'm not saying a word."

"Sixto," Balthazar said wearily, "we need a drink. We need two drinks. Very cold. And some food. We also need a swim and a lot of sleep. Which we are not going to get. But definitely the food. Take me to your feeder."

Sixto looked at him.

"It loses something in translation," Balthazar said sheepishly.

Glancing around the small outdoor restaurant, Balthazar decided it wasn't his idea of a Parisian sidewalk café, but it wasn't a bad substitute. He and Sixto sat at a small plastic table near the sidewalk. The quiet street was lined with oleander bushes, starred with white flowers. The sun, setting behind the surrounding tall buildings, pulled the day's heat with it. The pale orange streetlights, just coming on, were the same color as the sky. Under the overhanging roof of the restaurant, a number of customers, mostly men, sat at a large horseshoe-shaped counter and joked with the waitresses.

Balthazar had ordered *churrasco*—a thin, very tender steak, served with a small pitcher of spices, garlic, and oil to pour over it, and a large helping of fresh avocados and tomatoes on rice. He tried one of the local beers. He decided he could definitely get used to them. They were all light, but with slightly more taste than most American beers.

"How do you like Haverford?" he asked as they finished. "Could have tied up his boat and done all three murders over the weekend. He's a loner, not attractive, enraged at both his adoptive mother and his real one, could hate women."

"He had not planned on killing the girl. Sexual frustration." Sixto sighed. "He strangles the other two to hide his crime."

Balthazar rubbed his knee. "Back to headquarters," he said.

The night clerk walked down the length of the long registration desk at the Dupont Plaza. He stopped in front of the mail slots. There was a white envelope lying on the desk, addressed only to BALTHAZAR MARTEN. No room number. He glanced around the crowded lobby.

It was almost midnight, but the evening show in the Zanzibar Lounge had just ended, and a number of people were waiting for the elevators across from him. The two doors to the casino, on either side of the elevator banks, were wide open and people streamed in and out. Some shouted noisily to friends to join them; some of the departing gamblers were rather quiet and undoubtedly disappointed by their luck. But there was no one near the desk who might have left the envelope.

The night clerk picked it up and frowned, then ran his finger down the list. He checked the registrations. No Balthazar Marten.

He tapped the envelope against his thumbnail. The day manager might know. There were several rooms reserved by the management that were occupied. People in those rooms didn't usually register. Best to hand it over to the day crew, he decided. He threw it on a pile of papers waiting for the morning shift. Then he sat down heavily. He wasn't due to go off work until the casino closed at 4:00 A.M., and he was already beat, answering questions about the attractions on the Condado and in Old San Juan for hotel guests still eager for nighttime entertainment. Plus the constant explanations about buses and taxis for sightseers planning for the next day. The hotel was almost full. It was always busy at the height of the tourist season.

6

IT HAD BEEN very late when Balthazar and Sixto left headquarters the previous evening and very early on Wednesday when they returned. But as they came off the elevator, they could see that the three people in the large, glass-boothed phone center at the entrance to the Criminal Investigation Corps were already swamped with incoming calls. All the buttons on the phones were blinking. As soon as one receiver was put down, that phone rang again.

Alvalos, a short, fresh-faced officer inside the booth, managed to grin at the two men and wave them over to him, while still scribbling busily with one hand and repeating assurances in a concerned voice into the phone. Yes, an officer would be out today, probably today, to take down the particulars of the strange man who had followed their daughter right into their driveway last night. Yes, he realized that the caller had found it impossible to get through to headquarters at the time. Yes, it was wise not to have burdened the emergency line. Yes, it probably was just someone who was drinking too much but it was well to report it. Yes, he had the address. He even thanked Señor Rios for calling. He put the message on top of a thick stack of others, which were scooped up by a policeman hurrying into the adjoining small radio center that broadcast to the agents in the field.

Balthazar listened to him, thinking that the River Rat case had been different. The public was not so alarmed when prostitutes were the killer's targets. Here they feared for their own families. And they wanted to help.

Alvalos held down the button on the receiver cradle and spoke to them through a slot in the glass. "Chief Villareal called from the Forensic Institute. He doesn't know when he'll be back, but he'd like to talk to everyone here later this afternoon. Also," he crinkled his face apologetically, "there are many new reports of interviews in the Investigation room—backlogs. Some of the agents couldn't find either time or an unused typewriter until early this morning." He put the receiver back to his ear, glared ferociously at the blue and white poster next to the desk which proclaimed that the *Policía* were honored to serve and protect the citizenry, waggled a finger over the lighted buttons, and punched one.

Balthazar and Sixto went down the narrow corridor that led to the Homicide Section. Unlike most of the hallways in the well-kept, modern building, this one had holes gouged in the drywall, black scuff marks on the paint. Some suspects had clearly been reluctant to go into the interrogation rooms on the edges of the Homicide Section, or even less willing to leave them to go to the cold, bare concrete holding cells at the other end of the corridor.

The Homicide Department was a large square room with windowed offices on one wall and dark interrogation rooms on the wall facing them. Steel and frosted glass partitions on the other two walls formed small offices, used when needed by both the Homicide One and Two detectives, who spent most of their days in the field. At that moment all of these areas were occupied by agents pounding typewriters, ignoring the phones ringing everywhere in the room.

Balthazar and Sixto looked around the crowded, noisy room, looked at each other and without a word, both of them wheeled around and headed for the small coffee machine on the other side of the phone center. Carrying their coffee, they opened the door to the spare meeting room set aside for this investigation. Two of the three long folding tables in the empty room had stacks of sorted reports. The third was buried under loose sheets. They put down their cups and began putting these into piles. Every relative and friend of the victims—in fact it seemed everyone who'd passed them on the street—had been interviewed. After reading these, the two detectives had to decide who needed to be reinterviewed. Given the urgency, the investigation had to be organized in this way, Balthazar realized, but it troubled him.

He needed to watch people as they talked, listen to their voices instead of reading what they said. Did their eyes shift left or right? What were they doing with their hands? Did they pause or answer immediately? The young classmates and friends—those who knew the dead girls best—might leave out revealing details, thinking them unimportant. He knew from past experience that sometimes they even fudged when answering, thinking they should protect the victim's reputation. "Oh, no, Officer, she would never stay out all night." Sometimes they protected their own, as if the police were also the guardians of morals.

There were typos, to be expected from tired, harried officers. "Susan often bent the car." Balthazar stopped. Loaned it to friends? Had fender benders? Called Hertz or Avis on occasion? And this was a bilingual society where people cheerfully mixed the languages. English and Spanish had thousands of common words, pronounced differently, which usually, but not always, meant the same thing. Often you had to know what someone was talking about, and in which language, before you understood what was said. *Aquí* meant "here" in Spanish, but sounded exactly like "a key." And then the college students' English was full of current slang. The officer taking quick notes might be unfamiliar with the expressions, or his own knowledge of mainland vernacular, dating back to a period perhaps twenty years earlier when he'd lived there, confused the issue.

Karen Hoover's boyfriend, Marc Kimball, had described the girl as "cool." Did that mean she was a reserved girl, unlikely to talk to strangers? Agent Gonzalez, who had interviewed him, hadn't asked, perhaps assuming the young man was saying something complimentary about her. Furthermore, was Marc implying a possible motive when he stressed that Karen had a large trust fund or was he merely stating a fact, or perhaps even bragging that he was dating a very rich girl? They'd have to talk to him themselves. Balthazar scribbled notes to himself.

There was a quick knock, and a head with the Cheshire Cat's grin peered around the door. "Honno," Sixto said with pleasure, "come in. You have not yet met Lieutenant Marten. This is Alejandro Gallo, technically our Police Audio-Visual Specialist. He also handles our press relations."

Gallo was a plump, darkly handsome man with a sculpted black beard and wide, gentle blue eyes. He was wearing a rumpled *guayabera* and well-worn comfortable sandals. "Yes, I deal with the gentlemen," he stressed the word ironically, "of the press. That was not part of the job description when they hired me," he added mournfully, shaking hands with Marten.

"His office is full of shouting reporters, but Señor Gallo never complains and he always remains calm," Sixto said, laughing.

"Of course, Cardenas. I simply remember my Kipling. 'If you can trust yourself when all men doubt you,/Something, something, something/If you can keep your head when all about you/Are losing theirs. . . .' you have a rat turd for a brain. Right now I have a message for the lieutenant. The Secretary of Justice asks that you join him at today's press conference."

Balthazar winced. "I've nothing new to say."

"Neither," Gallo responded wryly, "does he. He asks that you meet him at five-thirty this afternoon in my office for a preconference conference. He managed to put the press off until six o'clock. You will be on the ten o'clock local news. And the newspapers can spend the night analyzing what you didn't say."

"Are this morning's papers in yet?"

"Yes, I can give you a brief summary. They are printing what the Secretary didn't say yesterday. They approve of the fact that the university has canceled its night classes and activities and has doubled its security force. They urge the public to remain calm, asserting that the *Policía* will catch the Strangler. All of them, except *El Clamor*, of course. They insist we are baffled, that we are not taking rigorous measures, that the FBI must be called in, the Air National Guard must be alerted—"

"The Air National Guard?" Sixto asked incredulously.

"Of course, foolish man. So that they can fly over the city, constantly keeping an eye out for the Strangler as they streak by at six hundred miles an hour." He gave them both a dignified salute and left the room, almost bumping into Stan, short for Constanzia, a tall, slim woman detective, who was entering. She was carrying a sheaf of papers in one hand and a cookie in the other. Her hair, dark with a reddish tint, was cut stylishly, and her makeup was expertly applied, but it could not hide the dark circles of fatigue under her eyes. "Your mother called, Sixto, but I could see you were talking to Gallo," she said, nibbling at the praline cookie. "I told her these are the best *dulces de coco* I'd ever eaten. She sent these over last night with one of the patrolmen. I am eating the very last of that huge box. She gave me the recipe."

"I'd better call her." Sixto disappeared toward the phone center.

"You know," Stan waved the papers in her hand, "the newspapers are encouraging the citizens of San Juan to give every assistance to the police. In my view, this means they should be careful, but lead their usual happy lives. But the public assumes that they must report every odd occurrence on their street without thinking what possible connection it could have to these murders. Aargh!"

Balthazar grinned at her mock woebegone expression. Humor disguises tension the way caffeine suppresses exhaustion, he reflected. But the strain and the fatigue remain.

"Then," Stan continued grimly, "there was the wonderful editorial that said women should only go out after dark if accompanied by a *man*. I will use the figure four chokehold on the next guy in this department who offers to protect me through the night."

Sixto came back, running his fingers through his hair. "My mother believes that if you are not getting enough sleep, you must eat much more. So today she and Cousin Ida are going to make *empanadillas* for us. Some with crab, some with beef. At the price of crab and beef, I will have to eat only rice and beans for dinner until the day I retire. But they make very good pastries."

Balthazar finished a page of one of the last reports, drained his fourth cup of coffee, and gingerly bent his knee back and forth to make sure it wouldn't lock when he stood up. "I see I am on the third page of this and I haven't read a word. Let's go and talk to the Hoover girl's baseball coach and boyfriend. We can compare notes on the way."

"*Sí.* I would feel better if we were out in the city, as I usually am. It does not seem as if I am working fast enough, sitting here. I'm nervous and at the same time . . . wrung up."

"Out," Balthazar said.

"Good idea," Sixto responded.

As they walked through the police parking lot, Balthazar said, "You know, on our way back we could stop by your house, pick up the hot *empanadillas*, and bring them with us, stuffing ourselves as we drive."

Sixto sighed. "The uniformed branch has already selflessly volunteered to get them."

***

Dolores Vann's office at the university gymnasium was Spartan, gray, and functional. Filing cabinets crowded her steel desk. One off-white wall had ten narrow-framed photographs of young women in baseball or basketball uniforms. One rather yellowed shot showed a pitcher for the Wacs, throwing underhand, a much younger, smiling version of Coach Vann.

She herself was economical in her movements and at first laconic in her replies to their questions. A compact woman in her early forties, her muscles were taut beneath the shorts she was wearing. Her graying brown hair was cut shorter than either of the two men's.

"You're interested in my whereabouts over the weekend, Lieutenant?" Her smile was slightly bitter. "Simply put, I was working. Money for women's sports is limited here. The cash—and the glory—go to men's athletics. Consequently, I coach three sports. Baseball is a year-round sport here and very popular—even women's baseball. There's also basketball and gymnastics."

Balthazar sensed the woman's tension, as though she was constantly clenching her entire body. Yet she made no nervous gestures. The only item on her desk, besides a graceful spray of fuchsia bougainvillea in a pewter vase, was a silver whistle on a long chain. She placed it carefully in a top drawer. A slight flat drawl from somewhere in the South contrasted oddly with her precise enunciation.

"Saturday evening I was exhausted. I always am. I had dinner with a friend and spent the night at her home. Her name is Ana Castro, if you wish to ask her."

She looked for a long moment at Balthazar, then spoke dryly. "Yes, Lieutenant, your worst fears are confirmed. She is my lover. We went out to brunch Sunday morning, and then I came here. She met me later and we attended the baseball game. We left together. *Before* Karen's body was discovered. I understand that the police have been questioning quite a few members of the gay community. Since I have already been interviewed by the police, I can only assume that the reason you are here is that I am known to be a lesbian."

Although her movements were still controlled, her hazel eyes were angry. "In my view, it is unthinkable that one's sexual preference should cause one to be automatically suspected of murder. Particularly of the murder of one's own students. Particularly of a girl whom I liked and whose abilities I admired. She played baseball as if it mattered to her. Some of my women students are afraid of breaking their nails. Karen and I would occasionally have lunch together; she often assisted me in refereeing basketball or umpiring baseball games. She herself was not homosexual. She dated one of the men students regularly. In fact, the only thing I know to her discredit was her choice of that young man. He is in love only with himself. Now, if you will excuse me—my next class in calisthenics is due to begin."

Halfway through the interview with Marc Kimball, Balthazar began to have a sharp fellow feeling with Ms. Vann. He didn't like Karen's boyfriend either. He was dressed in a tight T-shirt and purple satin shorts and he walked restlessly around his cramped dormitory room as if before a spellbound audience of women spectators at a body-building competition, just stopping short of striking poses. Kimball was very well built, with broad shoulders, narrow waist and hips, and rock-hard thighs and calves. His short curly hair was blond, and thick blond hairs covered his muscular forearms. He answered their questions without hesitation, looking at the two detectives with a direct blue gaze.

Saturday afternoon he had had soccer practice and then had gone out with some of the other team members for a few beers. He couldn't remember what time the practice session had broken up or how long it took him to get to the bar. Saturday night he and Karen had gone to the Carolina Mall to catch the latest Eddie Murphy flick at seven o'clock. Perhaps someone would remember him. He wasn't sure what time they got back to the campus since they'd sat in the car and talked awhile. Sunday night he dropped in on Karen's game but didn't stay because he had a sociology exam on Monday morning. He sat with a friend of his, didn't know what time he left the game. His friend might remember. He had not talked to Karen on Sunday night. He had been in his room with the door open—other students had seen him. He realized, of course, that they had to check everything and everybody.

"In your previous interview," Balthazar remarked as if it were an afterthought, "you mentioned that Karen had a large income."

"Big bucks. Not that she threw money around. She could have had a Ferrari, but guess what she drove? A little Mitsubishi." Kimball shook his head, with a quick glance at them as if he were sure the two men would share his disbelief. "We could have hopped around the Caribbean—St. Martin, Martinique, St. Thomas—sailed, wind-surfed, gambled a little, had some fun. She said no. She wanted to be a coach later, but first she was going to try a little semipro ball. Can you believe it? Who cares about women's sports? But we had to hang out here—she always had practice or some game or other."

He'd sat down briefly on the plaid bedspread that covered the narrow bed. The two detectives were sitting on the two chairs, that with a student desk and dresser, comprised the furnishings. The room was cluttered with athletic equipment. Baseball bats, balls, and cleats, a black and white soccer ball, a squashed-in basketball, tennis rackets and cans of balls, six or seven different kinds of athletic shoes were jumbled in the corners. A surfboard leaned near the open closet, and a big pile of sweat socks, grass-stained shorts and T-shirts that Marc had swept off the chairs lay on the closet floor. At the foot of the unmade bed were several bars with different sized weights attached. Marc stood up again as if his muscles ached at inactivity. He idly hefted one of the weight bars with one hand, raising and lowering it as he talked. "You'd have thought her folks kept her on as tight a budget as mine do. Her mom was dead. I thought the way Karen looked when she mentioned it that it might have been . . . suicide."

He pursed his lips and shook his head again. "She had a stepmother but she never talked about her. Now, her dad was, how can I put it? Just weird. He'd call once in a while, always late at night, and I could tell from her end of the conversation that he was drunk. She'd always end up crying, but she wouldn't talk about it. Just sit there, tears running down her face but not making any noise. I'd just leave her alone. You know how women get.

"You know, I even wondered—" He paused, looking thoughtfully first at the weight and then at the two men. Their quiet attention encouraged him. "Well, like if, I say *if*, her father needed money and well, if she died, he'd get hers, wouldn't he? Really rich people always tie up their money so it stays in the family. Karen said that once about her trust fund. And I guess he doesn't work or anything—all the money came from his great-grandparents. So he could hire a hit man maybe, and if the guy was smart, he'd kill the other girls to cover up that it was really Karen he was after."

He put down the weight again and perched on the edge of the bed, his hands clasped in front of him, arms resting on his powerful thighs, squinting at them intently. "You look like the right guys to mention this to. I thought I'd better bring it up—being an insider, I'd be the only one who might think of it."

Balthazar nodded, his face blank. "We would have to consider that. You probably are the only one who would think of it."

Sixto leaned forward, and said conversationally, "We have a report that says six months ago you beat up the girl you were living with."

"What?" Marc jumped to his feet in one quick motion. "That's not true, that's not the way, who said—"

"Sit down," Balthazar said coldly. He tapped his clipboard. "The girl was taken to the university hospital with a skull fracture and bruises on her jaw and neck. At the time, she said you struck her, but later didn't press charges. Nonetheless, the Security Department here was informed."

Marc shot an outraged glance at Sixto, shifting from the ball of one foot to the other. Sixto looked back at him impassively.

Lowering the weight, he sank back down on the edge of the bed. "She fell and hit her head. That's all. We were arguing. God, that girl was such a nag, a first-class bitch, and she wouldn't shut up. I might have given her a little . . . push, but I didn't choke her, for God's sake."

They stood up. He remained seated, glowering at the floor.

"We're going to check every minute of your weekend, Kimball," Balthazar assured him. "You'd better hope that your friends have better memories for times than yours."

Their brown Chevy Nova had been baking in the sun. Balthazar pushed his dark hair back from his forehead, leaned his head back, and stretched his legs. "I don't like him at *all*."

"Well," said Sixto slowly, "he *could* have slipped out—"

"What?" said Balthazar, sitting up. "No, I meant he's a real. . . . Still, look at what Karen's teammates say about Sunday night. There's something odd there." He opened his notebook and flipped through the pages clipped together at the top.

Sixto, watching him, stirred uneasily. "I have been meaning to ask. You write down so much. And yet your memory is very good. In my notebook, sometimes I just . . . doodle obscenely. Perhaps I should begin—"

"Probably just my early training—compulsive Dutch aunt, strict nuns." He stopped turning the pages and added, "But in this kind of case, I try for a pattern. I have to pull things out of different places in my mind and write them down, put them together. You know, as if these memories are on separate floppy disks. Then, when I recall a conversation or even someone's expression, something unlikely that's right next to it in the storage bank pops up. Sometimes that works. Strange. Do you ever think of your memory as a computer that somebody *else* programmed?"

"No," Sixto said, "I do not think so."

Balthazar put his finger on the next page. "Here we are. The other players said everyone was pretty quiet after the game—they lost—and they straggled back to the gym. But Karen was feeling pretty good—at least she had ended her batting slump with a couple of good hits. Let's see . . . Um . . . they think several people stopped her. . . . Um . . . one girl remembers a guy with a camera around his neck—clean-shaven, glasses, probably a reporter. . . . Yes, here it is. Another girl said that Karen spent some time putting on makeup after her shower, but she figured it was a date with Marc, even though he says they had no plans."

He glanced at Sixto. "That is kind of interesting, you know."

Sixto looked at him blankly.

"If we assume she was just going back to the dorm, and the Strangler surprised her, why bother with makeup?"

Sixto stared at the steering wheel. "They do not always do this?"

"Not if she were just going to bed. I—"

The radio chattered to life. Chief Villareal would like them to return in an hour for a conference. The dispatcher's cool voice added, "The hotel manager says he has a message for you, Lieutenant Marten."

Balthazar frowned. Why would New York call the hotel instead of headquarters? "Oh, it's probably MacAtee. An old friend of mine in New York. He's the only one I gave the phone number to. He probably," he added wryly, "just wants to inquire about the tourists' bikinis."

"These string bikinis . . ." Sixto began.

"I've heard." Balthazar said. "We've still got time to talk to the janitor at the gym who found the Hoover girl's body. He should be on duty now."

Hector Lopez was squat, unshaven, and smelled of the antiseptic he'd been mopping the floor with. He was sweating even in the cool gymnasium.

"Sorry to trouble you again, Señor Lopez," Balthazar began, "just checking a few details. You say you noticed

Miss Hoover leaving the gym after the game and as far as you recall she was alone?"

"*Sí*, Señor."

The janitor pushed the mop handle up and down in the bucket nervously, splattering water on the stone floor that surrounded the polished wood of the basketball court. He stopped and took out a soiled handkerchief, wiped his perspiring brow, and blew his nose juicily. He kept his eyes fixed on the framework of the clear plastic backboard and the hoop over their heads.

But he seemed to relax when he went through his familiar testimony about finding the body. He had just gotten off work at 2:00 A.M. and he was taking his usual shortcut behind the stadium. Then he saw the girl's legs, sticking out of the shrubbery. At first he had thought it was some kind of joke by the students. He looked closer, but he didn't touch the body; he hadn't even recognized the girl because of the darkness and the bushes. He ran back to the gym and immediately phoned the police.

They had asked him many, many questions. Did he know the other girl, where had he been on this night and that night. He had been at work, of course, his days off were Tuesday and Wednesday—the gym was used a lot on the weekends. Many people had seen him, including the campus police. That was all he could tell them. He was sorry he could not be of more help. He shrugged and spread his hands out, palms upward, his eyes wide.

Balthazar, recalling Lopez's initial uneasiness, leaned over the little man and almost barked out the next question: "How did you happen to notice that particular girl when she left the gym, Lopez?"

He backed away from the detective, gulping. "Because . . . because I know her. She referees the basketball games and she is here often. She had keys—"

"Most of the girls don't have keys?"

"Oh, no, no. Miss Vann, she is *muy* particular. The equipment room, the room for the balls, the gloves, for all the sports, she demands it be kept locked at all times."

Balthazar shoved the man against the yellow-tiled wall. The antiseptic smell didn't cover a bad body odor. "Do *you* have a key to the equipment room?"

Lopez spread his arms out, the tips of his fingers scrabbling at the tile. "No, no, Señor. Miss Vann, she had the lock changed. Only a very few people have keys."

"Why?"

"Because . . . because, some of the equipment has been missing."

"Even after the lock was changed?"

"*Sí*. But I tell Miss Vann over and over, it is just that the students do not always remember to return what they have used."

"She asks you a lot about it?"

"I am here by myself late at night. She would ask if anyone comes in."

"Karen Hoover talked to you about this stuff, too, right?"

"Not . . . not . . ." the man stammered, looking beseechingly at Sixto, as if for relief from this tall, menacing Anglo.

Sixto moved to the janitor's left side and, standing very near his ear, hissed, "I think she talked to you about it the night she died, Lopez. And you did not include it in your statement to the *Policía*. I think you are in much trouble. Very serious trouble."

"But . . . but I *told* the *Policía* she was alone. That is what they asked. I saw nothing . . . it could have nothing to do . . . she was in a hurry—"

Sixto's voice was still low, but very distinct. He paused between each word. "Did she talk to you before she left? Answer the question."

"No, no, not then, the second time—"

"She came back?" Balthazar and Sixto said it almost in unison.

"This job, Señors, I need it," Lopez said miserably. "I have a family. It was nothing to do with the killing, I swear. How could it? The man is crazy, no? All the girls left—I watched them. Then I just happened to try the door to the equipment room."

"No, Lopez, no." Balthazar shook his head. "You have a key. You have been selling some of this stuff. If we begin asking around, it will be easy enough to find out."

"*Sí*," he said. He slid down the wall, knocking over his bucket with a clatter that echoed through the empty gym. Dirty suds pooled on the floor. He sat slumped over, his face in his hands. "*Sí*. I gave my little Francisco an old glove once. An old one. Who would miss it? Then one of the bigger boys in my *urbanización*, he say he could sell such things. So I give him some now and then. Miss Vann, she changed the lock. I watched the girls who have keys. Finally, one leaves the one I need, I get a copy of it, and the next day I put her key back where she finds it."

Sixto grabbed the man by the shirt front and pulled him up, bumping his head deliberately against the tile as he jerked him upright.

"The night Señorita Hoover died. What happened? Tell us everything. Leave out nothing."

"She came back just as I was leaving the equipment room." Lopez gritted his stained teeth to keep them from chattering. "I was carrying nothing. . . . One must be very careful, but I was checking, thinking about what would not be missed for a while. She said she came to get a bat."

"A bat?" Sixto's fingers were still clenched on Lopez's collar.

"*Sí, sí*. But then she looks at me funny and says how did I get in? I say the door was left open by accident. She said nothing, but after she got the bat, she locked the door very carefully, and then she ran out—"

"What time was this?"

"Maybe nine o'clock, Señor. I don't know . . ."

Sixto rapped the janitor's head against the tile. Balthazar's voice was low but furious. "Nobody found a bat near her body. What did she say she wanted with the bat?"

Lopez almost wailed. "But she did not say. She said nothing, nothing but what I have said."

"You should have said it the first time. You will now come with us to headquarters and say it all *correctamente*." Sixto half-carried the little man by his collar out of the gym, shaking him occasionally like a rat as he went.

7

THE NEWS GIVEN out at the conference by Chief Villareal had not been good. That was clear from the faces of the other agents, hurrying out past Balthazar and Sixto, who were just arriving.

At the front of the long Investigation Room, whose tables had been arranged in a T-shape for the meeting, Oscar Montez was listening stolidly to Angel Negrón, who was gesticulating angrily as he made his points. Seeing Balthazar and Sixto, Negrón bit off his words, and pushed past them without a glance, his lips so compressed that the jagged scar on his cheek stood out like a raw, inexpert incision. Montez shrugged his broad shoulders and looked at Villareal. The chief turned to the two men and shook his head in disgust.

"We have the pathologist's full report on Imelda Torres. She was not the third victim, but the *first*. Probably killed on Friday, not Monday."

"But, surely—"

"No, Lieutenant. Not a question of incompetence. We have plenty of that, but not in this case."

Balthazar was startled at Villareal's instant defensiveness. Was it his presence that called up that response? But then he thought of the press coverage and flinched. Certainly *El Clamor* wouldn't miss this chance to remind the public of the Casera case and go on to imply that the *Policía* were not only corrupt, but incompetent as well. It wouldn't matter what the actual cause of the delay was, or who was at fault, if anyone. A reporter could stick to the facts and still manage to convey the notion that the most basic steps of the investigation were being bungled.

The chief was tapping a folder on the table. "The girl was found in a swampy area near the Loiza River. Open land, heavily overgrown. Already the land crabs, the birds, the insects, the rats, even the small fish had been busy. You saw the photos of the body. Outward signs—the skin especially—indicated a fairly recent death. But the doctor thought the stomach contents suggested otherwise. They were permeated with stomach acid. She had eaten baked codfish and fresh corn tart for her last meal."

Villareal fumbled in his shirt pocket, took out a lemon yellow Chiclet square and stared at it. Then he put it in his mouth.

"She was a healthy girl—taught aerobics classes in the evening at the university. Such a meal, even given the corn, should have been digested fairly quickly. Pathology asks us for more information. We find that she was at her job at the military base on Friday. The cafeteria there served, among other things, codfish and corn tart. She ate a late lunch with another woman, and yes, that's what they had.

"So, what did she do over the weekend? We don't know. Her mother, a verỹ, very excitable woman, started calling us late Friday. Her daughter was missing. At first, we did not even make a note. Many, many daughters are missing on Friday. And this little Imelda had told her mother earlier she might spend the weekend with a girlfriend in Mayagüez on the western side of the island. She didn't show up. Naturally, we think that very possibly she is with her boyfriend in some other place entirely."

He took the papers out of the folder and looked at them as if hoping this time, the news would be different—and better. "But she was, the pathologist thinks, spending the weekend stuffed in a freezer, quite dead. Or at least, it seems so now. He is checking with the cryogeny experts at the university to be precise about the effects of extreme cold on decomposition. And nothing under her nails, but a deep ridge on several fingers of both hands. It is troubling."

"Our killer went to a lot of trouble to hide this body," Balthazar said slowly, pulling out one of the metal chairs and sitting down, "so that he could dispose of it later where it wouldn't be found for some time. Only this body? Why? Does her death implicate him?"

"Or perhaps," Sixto suggested eagerly, "he intended to hide *all* the bodies. That is why he chose the Bay beach. He planned to return in a boat and put the body in the sea. He could not know our traffic policeman would come along that evening. Or that the janitor would stumble over the body of Señorita Hoover."

"That's a lot of coincidence." Balthazar rubbed his head. "Maybe too much. But he could have been killing for some time, and he's becoming careless. He may even, subconsciously, wish to be caught. That would explain why the three murders were done so close together."

"It is the idea that these are not the only murders that is so troubling," Villareal replied, patting all his pockets nervously, as if his hands on their own were still hoping to find a cigarette packet. "One cannot rule out coincidence. That surely led to the finding of the Torres girl. The surveying crew for the bridge were just rechecking. Otherwise, the body might not have turned up for months, if at all, and identifying a skeleton—"

He sat down heavily next to Balthazar. "We have our share of open files—unsolved cases. And we have many reports on missing girls from the past that will now have to be checked. A one-way ticket to New York is not expensive. A young woman has a fight with her parents or her boyfriend. She thinks angrily that she will go visit a friend or a cousin in the States. She gets a job, she stays. It's a long time before she sends a postcard." His restless hands, discovering only a Chiclet box, crushed it. "Some of those girls could be all bones now, or perhaps they are plump and happy in New York City. Who is to know?"

He scraped his chair around to face Balthazar. "Still, Lieutenant, you must admit that now we should turn to those facts at our disposal regarding these killers. I have already assigned priority to investigating those suspects who fit the pattern. Someone in the homosexual community may have noticed odd behavior. We've started to run a check on known sex offenders. That includes even those who exhibit themselves. Bah! Some of those men barely have enough courage to unzip themselves. But we must be thorough and at least we can set up routine lines of investigation."

That idea seemed to cheer the chief up slightly.

"I would like to check that Torres girl's background, however," Balthazar said thoughtfully. "It could be that only she was a problem for him."

"Perhaps," Villareal agreed hesitantly. "But she was an ordinary, hard-working girl. It is difficult to see how she could have been a threat to anyone. But *I* do not wish to talk to her mother again, ever. Talking to Señora Torres is not easy. She has told us, the press, and I am sure, God himself, that we are fools, that we are doing nothing useful to solve the case. She will appreciate a new audience. I'm sure she will tell you everything she knows." He looked at Balthazar in some sympathy.

"No-no-no-no-no, Officer."

Señora Torres was a small-boned, pear-shaped Hispanic woman with chipmunk cheeks and a gold-rimmed front tooth. She was sitting next to her younger daughter who, like her sister, was much darker skinned than the mother.

"My daughter Imelda, she would *never* have taken a ride with a man she did not know. Never. And why should she with such a nice car of her own? One that she took excellent care of. A Honda Civic. Yellow. Which the police have not yet found, even though I gave the license number. It was on her key chain, which you have not found either. It was a little tag with the license plate number. Always she had it in her purse. I said to her that was dangerous. Someone takes your purse, they can also steal your car. Better, she said, than being asked your plate number at the base and looking the fool when you can't remember it."

The small living room had two hard, orange Naugahyde couches and a woven straw rug. Several small tables were crowded with dusty plastic plants, snapshots framed in sea shells, and carved statues of wooden saints. On the TV set, between lighted candles, was the picture Balthazar had seen of Imelda in her graduation cap. The mother's eyes kept straying to the picture as if to make sure *that* at least was still there, and her well-shaped, surprisingly delicate hands were never still. She smoothed her dress across her large stomach, adjusted her glasses, wiped her eyes, patted her younger daughter's hand.

If, Balthazar thought, it comforted her to remember her older daughter as an inspiring teacher, a magnificent dancer, an employee that the U.S. Government was lucky to have, and as chaste as the Virgin as well, then he would not wish it otherwise. But it made it very hard to figure out how her body ended up in a swamp by the Loiza River.

"No-no. She was such a good girl. And taking computer classes to improve herself. Very religious. You need not only take my word for it. Ask the neighbors. And so good to others as well. She taught the exercises for women at the place to quit the drugs. I do not remember the name. For this, she took no money. Only a week ago, she found that one of the officers at the base—a very, very, high-ranking one, possibly an admiral—was related to that poor Mrs. Avenaz, or whatever, down the street. And Imelda was pleased because she thought maybe now the poor woman could get medical benefits. I can never bear to talk to the

woman myself. She took care of her crazy husband for so
many years, kept him in the house with the shutters always
closed, but you could hear him shouting. She finally became *loca* herself, never making any sense, going on and on
about her child when the whole street knows there was only
the two of them from the time they moved in. But my
Imelda, she would talk to the woman as if she were like us."

Señora Torres extended her arm and waggled her index
finger. "And to think that the police would ask these questions about Imelda's going about with men! As if Imelda
knew crazy men! Being an *Americano*, you will understand
that they will not solve the case in this way. No-no-no-no-
no! You listen to me, Officer, my Imelda was the best. . . ."

Balthazar listened patiently. If he were to get any information, he would have to ask the neighbors.

It was past midnight, but as they left headquarters and
drove through the cool, empty streets, Balthazar realized
that he was too on edge to sleep. He rubbed the muscles
clenched at the base of his skull and noticed the tight grip of
Sixto's fingers on the wheel. "Beer?" he suggested.

Sixto promptly flicked on the turn signal and, a few
minutes later, pulled into a parking space not far from a
small outdoor restaurant.

As they walked down the street, Balthazar glanced
through the open window of a shiny new Toyota. A young
couple shared the reclined front passenger seat. They were
both wearing blue jeans and their slim bodies were so
tightly pressed together it looked as if they were wearing the
same pair. The girl's arm encircled the boy's neck, their eyes
were closed, and their lips joined in an oblivious, passionate
kiss. They did not stir as the men went by, apparently un-
troubled by the fears of stalking murderers that gripped
their elders.

The only other sign of life on the deserted street was a
small black female dog, the indeterminate breed referred to
as a *sato*, a Puerto Rican terrier. Her coat was mangy, with
patches missing, her ribs showed, and her heavy teats al-

most dragged on the ground. But she eyed the two policemen with intelligent speculation before wheeling and disappearing into the darkness.

Balthazar inclined his head toward the Toyota. "During the day every single one of those well-polished Japanese cars are on the streets and highways at all times. At night, when they are parked, each one seems to have a boy and girl in it, kissing. You'd think their mouths would get tired. And, after an intensive three-day study, while I have been thinking of little else, I have decided that this island has the best-looking kids and the world's scruffiest dogs."

"Right priorities," Sixto grinned.

At the sound of their footsteps, the waitress, a middle-aged woman with dyed red hair and puffy eyes, peered out into the street apprehensively. She had been sitting, alone, on a stool inside the U-shaped counter, her back firmly against the wall. She smiled with obvious relief when she recognized Sixto, took their orders, brought them beer, and hurried into the kitchen.

They sat in companionable silence, gratefully sipping from the icy cans. A tiny lizard clung to a column with a row of warm yellow lights, designed to keep away insects. His quick tongue caught the small gnats that flew up, unaware of the bulb manufacturer's advertising.

The waitress set a thick roll filled with pink layers of ham and melted cheese before Balthazar and a fat club sandwich before Sixto. She returned with a platter of fresh, golden fried potatoes, and then disappeared into the kitchen.

Balthazar set down his beer, stared at the lizard for a moment, and then said, "Angel Negrón. Have I somehow gotten in his way, taken over what should have been his job?"

Sixto took a bite out of his sandwich. "No," he said briefly.

"He's just got something against New Yorkers?" Balthazar persisted.

"No." Sixto put his sandwich down. "Negrón's a *mal-entraña*—even his insides are bad. But he thinks he's a good detective. And some of the men admire him."

"Looks like somebody doesn't—that cut on his face is fairly recent."

"A *puta*—a prostitute." Sixto looked away. "Negrón has a habit of causing them trouble. One had a razor concealed in her mouth."

"Then she had a bad fall—drunk, of course—and now she's in the hospital."

Sixto said nothing.

"He's been on the force awhile?"

Sixto nodded. "He came here from the military. I heard that at first he insisted on each thing by the rules. I think he was raised in an orphanage, by the sisters. But now—" Sixto angrily jabbed a french fry into the catsup on his plate. "And he gets out of the trouble he gets into. The Bureau of Special Investigations thought he might have been involved in the Casera case, but there was no evidence."

"I read something about that case. A couple of cops were accused of killing her. How?"

"Stick against the neck." Sixto demonstrated.

"Pretty effective," Balthazar remarked.

"The two officers," Sixto said reluctantly, "who are suspected in this case—they have not come to trial yet. I knew them a little. One would not have thought—"

He went on, but he obviously wanted to change the subject. "We say the devil knows more from experience than from being the devil. And some men's experience teaches them the wrong thing. When I was at the police academy, I wanted to do all things right. I practiced and practiced shooting. I am a very good shot. But to be a good policeman, I found that one must not . . . jump to the gun. People act *estúpido*, they get a little drunk. One must try to be patient."

Balthazar smeared the moisture on the can with his thumb. "Suppose we never catch the Strangler. In the Casera case a good defense lawyer could raise a reasonable doubt in the jury's mind by suggesting that Teresa Casera was another of the Strangler's victims, that those two cops are innocent. Not quite the same method, but close. Teresa Casera must have been about the same age as these girls. The prosecution could stress motive in her case, but still, with all the publicity on these recent killings, the jury would be bound to be influenced."

"We will catch this man," Sixto said, picking up his sandwich.

"Yes," Balthazar replied firmly, "we will." He ordered two more beers and stared at Sixto's sandwich. "I will never get used to the idea of a fried egg on a club sandwich."

"It is very good that way and," Sixto said, studying it with appreciation, "much like the breakfast at Burger King."

Balthazar took the elevator directly from the downstairs parking lot where Sixto had dropped him to avoid the congestion of taxis in front of the hotel, which were picking up and letting out tourists enjoying their vacations by partying late. He went straight to his room on the tenth floor.

The night desk clerk was watching for a man of his description. The manager had said that Señor Marten was a policeman and the envelope might be an important message and should be delivered personally. So the clerk scanned the lobby conscientiously when he was not busy. But in any case, the small red light on the room phone was lit. Señor Marten would know there was a message.

Balthazar clicked on the bedside lamp and saw the red light on the phone. He yawned—it was almost 2:00 A.M., much too late to call MacAtee. He turned the phone to face the other bed and fell asleep instantly.

His sleep was troubled. In his dream, rows of young women were propped against a whitewashed wall. Their heads hung limply, at odd, sickening angles.

Another woman was walking away in the distance. He hurried after her; she had to be warned. Although she was not walking fast, he had enormous difficulty catching up to her. Finally he reached out and caught his fingers in her long hair. The softest hair, with glints of sun.

She turned. On both of her wrists there were gardenia corsages. It was Maira Knight, but this time she was smiling at him warmly.

They were standing by a gray steel desk in an unfamiliar office. Phones rang, and faceless strangers bustled about. He lifted his arms and put his hands on her shoulders.

She still smiled, but he knew he shouldn't be touching her. He could not stop. His longing to caress her was intense. Only a moment longer, he thought. He could not swallow or breathe. Only a moment longer. People would soon notice them. And then he would let her go. But just now he could not. He moved closer, and he never wanted to wake up. He wanted to stay in the dream.

He woke wet, sweating, entranced.

8

Sixto Cardenas was surprisingly cheerful that morning.

He had had only four hours of sleep, and it had seemed more like five minutes. All he had eaten for breakfast was the fresh doughnut his mother had thrust into his hand as he left, instead of the omelet she had urged on him, following him out to the car. Traffic on the way to the Condado had been ferocious. Sweating at each stoplight, he had willed it to turn green. Once in the Tourist Zone, on that thin strip of land between the ocean and the Condado Lagoon, there was almost always the cool relief of the persistent trade winds. But now there was no breeze at all. The sky was overcast, and the air had so much moisture that one almost felt one could grasp it and wring it out.

It was likely that he would have to spend a long afternoon in court on a drug case that had ended in homicide and had been dragging on for weeks. He would even have to testify, which always made his stomach ache. The thought of taking any time away from the Strangler investigation made him squirm as if he had ants on his legs. All week, he had been consumed with a desperate urgency that both exhausted him and keyed him up. No one at headquarters could talk sensibly about anything but this case, and they all seemed to have something to say, huddling together in small groups, laughing nervously at the slightest joke, then hurrying off. And everyone was thinking that the killings took place on a weekend. Now another weekend was almost here.

But Sixto was not disheartened.

He was working with Lieutenant Marten, who said to call him Balthazar, but that didn't seem. . . . Marten was an expert in such cases, as the newspapers repeated each time they printed an interview with him. Yet he asked Sixto a lot of questions and listened carefully to the answers. The Lieutenant himself was not a talkative man, but he made Sixto think of why people said what they said, did what they did.

Pay attention, the Lieutenant urged, to what people *don't* say, too. If they've got something they don't want to tell you, sometimes they give that away without knowing it. Remember, they talk with their bodies, too—their eyes, their hands, the way they stand.

Now, Sixto thought, brushing doughnut crumbs from his lap, he would remember that. Then he remembered, too, what the Lieutenant had added. "Our understanding of body language is influenced by cultural ideas. I read that one anthropologist from Harvard noted that Anglo males rarely gesture with their hands while talking. Other groups, the French, the Italians, the Hispanics, move their hands, their arms, their whole bodies, in normal conversation. When Anglos who don't understand the spoken language see that, they consider those gestures feminine and, by extension, homosexual."

Sixto noticed that he himself was developing a tendency of late to keep his own hands loosely clasped behind his back.

The Lieutenant's determination to read every report, talk to every person involved in this case was amazing. It was also impossible. A dedicated man, Sixto thought, as well as a man of control. Not, he mused as he pulled into the hotel driveway, always running here and there like a. . . .

At that moment, Balthazar came racing down the wide outdoor staircase, hopping on his stiff knee, narrowly avoiding a collision with a party of Japanese tourists and the bellboy carrying their suitcases. He was holding up a plastic bag, with a sheet of paper in it.

He climbed hurriedly into the car and held it out for Sixto to read. It was in English and printed in block capitals.

YOU ARE A COCKSUCKING MFER NEW YORKER WHO DOESN'T KNOW HOG SHIT. BLOW IT OUT YOURS ASSHOLE. YOUR AS USELESS AS THREE TITS. THERE ARE MORE THAN THREE. I CAN DO 4 YOU TOO. TELL THEM YOU WANT OFF. EVEN CRAZY I AM GOOD. I CAN BLOW YOU AWAY WITH A BEAN SHOOTER AT A CLICK.

Sixto read it, and read it again. "From him, you think, the Strangler?"

"Seems likely."

"Because of the four?"

"He has to be referring to the figure four chokehold. And we have not released that information."

"He does not sound really Puerto Rican," Sixto said slowly. "Still, all Puerto Ricans know those English words. They know them in Spanish, too. But why does he send the message to you?"

"My name in the paper, maybe. What bothers me is how he knew where to find me. No one except Headquarters knows where I'm staying. And the manager said no one inquired—the message was left the night before last at the front desk. The clerk saw no one."

***

"That is disturbing," Villareal agreed, frowning at a photocopy of the note. Balthazar and Sixto sat next to each other in his office, facing the chief's desk. The chairs had the same green imitation-leather upholstery and metal legs as those scattered throughout the department, but these had padded arm rests. The polished wooden top of his desk had neat piles of manila folders and a stack of loose reports, edges squared. There was also a small trophy surmounted by a bronze golf ball.

This, a framed photograph of the *Superintendente* of the *Policía* shaking hands with Villareal, and a poster of a recent golf tournament at the Dorado-Cerromar Beach Hotel courses, were the only personal items. Administrative charts hung on two of the walls above bookcases crammed with fat reference volumes. The narrow windows overlooked a dark green river with one-story factories on its farther side. In the distance there was a clump of a hill surmounted by a huge, futuristic telephone microwave tower. Here the ringing of the phones was muffled. The room was cool, neat, and characterless.

Villareal looked up at last. "It means that he is watching *us*. That he recognized you from newspaper photos and followed you. And, to deliver it to the hotel—he is demonstrating how clever he is."

"Too clever for fingerprints, I'm sure," Balthazar said, rubbing his chin. "And he knows that about the only thing handwriting experts can tell from block capitals is whether the writer is right- or left-handed. Still, there are several things about that note that indicate he relies on his cleverness a great deal. He's not a detail person, not really careful. But not crazy, either."

Villareal's face was impassive. "We will see what a psychiatrist makes of it. There are several terms that I do not understand."

"Well, I think that 'click' is military slang for 'kilometer,' but we should have a language expert look at it. Someone who specializes in American slang."

"Yes," Villareal agreed, smoothing the edges of his mustache around the corners of his mouth. "But I am not so sure that the Strangler is not crazy, Lieutenant. And the note seems full of anger against you personally. The man is dangerous. Your name is in the newspaper on Tuesday morning, and already by late Tuesday night he finds you."

He stood up and walked to the window, his back to them. Without turning, he said slowly, "Perhaps it would be wise if we released a notice to the press that you were recalled to New York urgently. And," he paused tactfully, "there you could work with the FBI if they enter the case, and it would be an advantage for us."

Balthazar jumped up, bumping his knee on the desk as he strode to the window to stand next to the chief. "No," he said, more loudly than he meant, rubbing his knee in agony. "I would prefer staying here and on this case. The man is expressing anger, but it may not be directed at me personally. He may hate *Americanos* or just . . . authority figures, and he might simply transfer that feeling to another policeman. My name was probably just one of those he could pull from the newspaper articles. Perhaps other letters will follow—to you, to other officers involved in the investigation. If we allow him to think he can influence us to any degree, he may begin thinking he's really all-powerful. That could bring on more killings."

Villareal said nothing; he leaned over, craning his neck. From the far window one could catch part of the scene across the street in the Coliseum parking lot. With the brightly-painted television vans, the balloon sellers, the food vendors, and the crowds, it looked like an impromptu fiesta. The noise, however, was shut out by the windows, sealed off because of the air conditioning. There were only faint echoes from the street.

"But also," Balthazar pressed his point, "the press wouldn't believe that I'd been recalled. Not now. You wouldn't want to release the story on this note. The reporters would have a field day speculating on why I left. *El Clamor* would surely insist I was unhappy with the way the investigation was run, or worse. Allegations like that would only add to the public's panic." Villareal still did not face him, but Balthazar noticed a twitch in his jaw muscles.

Balthazar walked back to his chair, this time carefully avoiding the edge of the desk. Villareal turned and resumed his own seat. He opened the top drawer of his desk, filled with layers of boxes of Chiclets in different flavors. He considered for a moment, chose a box of spearmint, opened it, shook out four green squares, and, cupping his hand, popped them in his mouth as if they were pills.

Balthazar continued, "Look, I spend most of my time where a number of frightened citizens would like to be—here at headquarters, safely surrounded by armed policemen."

Villareal carefully closed the tab on the chewing gum box, laid it precisely on top of the other boxes, and closed the drawer. He spread his fingers apart, put one hand on each side of the stack of folders, and nudged an invisible imperfection in their alignment. His heavy-lidded eyes were fixed on the desk top. Balthazar gestured at Sixto, who brushed his dark hair nervously off his forehead. "The rest of the time I'm with Cardenas. Believe me, we'll be careful."

"You must be," Villareal said, still sounding unconvinced. "We will take special precautions. You must change your residence. I will send someone for your clothing. Take cars only from the police parking lot—" Villareal paused, "—and then only if they have been checked. We should discuss this again later."

He opened a file folder. "But for the moment, we have here the statement from Susan McKinley's friend with the boat. John Havorford, yes? The lawyer who came with him did all the saying, but apparently the young man has a beachfront house in Rincón, also. Now that is interesting. Rincón is very near Mayagüez—where the Torres girl was supposedly going. Rincón is famous for its surfing beaches; young Haverford surfs. And, yes, there is a large freezer in that house. We will have the Mayagüez police examine it very carefully.

"And a man named Erik Janssen, apparently a homosexual, was in some trouble yesterday in the Tourist Zone. He gave John Haverford as a reference. Perhaps you would like to talk to Janssen."

***

As they drove, Balthazar skimmed the contents of the file Villareal had given him. But he looked up as the car pulled onto Dos Hermanos Bridge, the broad connecting link between Old San Juan and the Condado, the tourist zone. On his right, the dark blue lagoon was ruffled gently by the light wind that had blown away the overcast. On his left, the Atlantic rushed against the heavy rocks that protected swimmers at the small public beach at one foot of the bridge. Tourists in bright clothes strolled the wide sidewalks, obviously enjoying the sparkling air. Young men sat on the low balustrade of the bridge staring avidly at the girls on the beach.

They drove off the bridge and onto Avenida Ashford, the palm-lined street that winds down the Condado. The towering luxury hotels, interspersed with designer shops and expensive jewelry stores, were on the Atlantic side. But just across the street on the lagoon side, there was much more of a mixture of building styles—and levels of prosperity. Modern glass apartment buildings stood next to what had once been private mansions. Some of these were maintained beautifully, some were in the process of restoration, others were crumbling, filled with crowded minimarkets, massage parlors, pizza places, and unpretentious outdoor cafes. Balthazar was surprised at the number of foot patrolmen, all wearing gold-embroidered Tourist Zone patches on their sleeves. As Sixto pulled into an open parking lot that sloped to the lagoon, Balthazar commented on the overwhelming presence of the police.

"*Sí*," Sixto said, "tourism is very important to us."

"Of course, but seeing this makes the report on Janssen more understandable. Let me fill you in before we talk to him. It has its humorous side."

He looked at the file. "This middle-aged tourist couple stopped one of the officers right along here. She complains that a homosexual harassed them in one of these sidewalk bars. She points it out. She's pretty upset, and she says, 'Officer, that man even touched my husband's body.' The officer says, 'Where?' And she screams, "Right there, right there in that bar. I just showed you!'"

Balthazar grinned at Sixto.

Sixto looked back at him uncertainly.

"See," Balthazar began, "the patrolman asks *where* the guy . . . Never mind. Anyway, the officer calls another one over and they go talk to the guy. He's pretty big, curly blond hair. They don't like his answers at all, so they hustle him into the nearest taxi. . . . A taxi?"

"*Sí*. Sometimes. Not to upset the tourists. They do not wait for a patrol car—they just take them away quickly."

"Okay. But when they shove him into the taxi, his hair falls off. It's a wig. Guy's really got short dark hair—military haircut. Turns out he's a sailor stationed at Roosevelt Roads Naval Base. Been in the service for ten years—since he was eighteen. Electronics technician. They let him off with a warning. But he says he's staying with a friend on the Condado and the friend's at present in New York. So they ask for references and he names Haverford, whose apartment is a couple blocks down from here, right?"

The address Janssen had given was that of a four-story mansion whose graceful curving art deco facade clearly dated back to the late twenties. The cracks on the outside had been patched, and painters were at work on its pale beige exterior. As they approached, a tall, muscular blond, dressed in a sleeveless black T-shirt and white pants, was inserting a key in the outside door, a brown grocery bag tucked under one arm.

"Petty Officer Janssen?" Balthazar hazarded. "We'd like to talk to you a moment."

The man carefully put down the sack on the concrete step, his handsome face hardening into a frown. He moved like an athlete.

"What about?"

When they produced their identification, his frown deepened.

"As long as you're going in," Balthazar said, "perhaps it'd be better if we talked inside."

They followed him up the broad staircase to the top floor. Although the building had been split into four separate units, the marble staircase with its curving dark mahogany rail had been lovingly restored.

The man opened the penthouse door and they followed him inside. Both Balthazar and Sixto stared. The living room was white. White walls, white couches, white chairs, even the wooden floor was washed in white. But hanging on all the walls the bright, primitive paintings of Haiti threw color around the huge room like prisms. Tropical reds, clear yellows, hummingbird greens, unimaginable blues. The paintings were reflected in the glass tables, the chrome fixtures, the mirrors. Here and there, perfectly matched small pillows picked up the colors.

The man seemed to relax, enjoying their reaction. "My friend," he stressed the word slightly, "and I really indulged ourselves in decorating. Only the best of the Haitian painters. Some of them have gone up just amazingly in price. But 'Pricio—he's Capriccio Caro, the designer you know—right now he's at his place in Manhattan. I'm here on my lonesome. But only here can I feel my true self, let out the real me."

He waved his long arm expansively, smiled for the first time, and motioned them to a couch. He started to seat himself opposite across one of the glass tables, but then stopped.

"But what am I thinking of? You must need some refreshment. I know I do. Let me get us a tray."

"That's quite all right," Balthazar raised a hand. "Please sit down. Just a few questions, Petty Officer. . . ."

"Nonsense, nonsense. And my friends call me Rik. No 'C.'" With a nod at Sixto's open notebook, he disappeared into the kitchen.

Sixto raised his eyes to the ceiling.

Rik returned almost immediately. "The water will be hot in just a tick. I had it all nice and boiling before when I realized I was out of the jasmine. I never take caffeine, of course. All wrong for you, you know. So I hurried out. Now, if you'll just excuse me one quick thought more, I need to change." He disappeared into the bedroom.

Balthazar rose and moved to the window. Below lay the lagoon, its surface dotted with the multicolored, triangular sails of the wind-surfers. The man's sudden change in behavior was unsettling. At the front door, he gave the impression of power, of control. But once inside, his mannerisms became exaggerated. Balthazar wondered if what he had said about "the real me" was the simple truth. Or rather the complex truth. Janssen, as a homosexual and an enlisted man, would need to put up an elaborate front before the world at all times. The military tried hard to get homosexuals out of the ranks. But a number managed to get in and stay in, attracted not only by the presence of other men, but by the order, the careful structure of such a life. If a man was talented, and there was no overt homosexual behavior, the military pretended a lack of interest in his sexual preference.

One of the wind-surfers slipped off the narrow board and the brilliant sail lay flat in the water. The surfer struggled desperately to right it. As soon as he got the sail vertical, it flopped over onto the other side before he could climb back on the narrow plank.

The trouble, Balthazar reflected, was that he himself could not really interpret homosexuals' body language. Their imitation of feminine behavior was sometimes almost overdone, a parody of womanly movements. Did they mean in fact to parody women? Or was it that they just couldn't get it right? No narrow-hipped man could ever catch the easy sway of a woman's wider pelvis. Balthazar stared down at some of the spectacular pelvises on the sunbathing women below.

It would be necessary, he decided, to let the man talk, listen to him carefully.

Rik returned in a very short silk robe, tightly belted. It made his extreme height even more evident. His calves and thighs were long, the muscles firm, and they were completely hairless. His blond curls were carefully arranged. He grinned at them hospitably, and went through the white swinging doors to the kitchen.

The lacquer tray he set before them was solid black except for a line or two of gold. The tiny cups, the teapot, the sugar bowl were stark white. Six delicate slices of lemon lay on a white plate. And in a white bowl, a yellow double hibiscus floated.

"I always think," Janssen said, pulling down his robe as he perched on the edge of the couch, "that there is nothing as fragrant as jasmine. One feels as if one were swallowing an aroma, not a taste. Now then."

He handed a cup to Balthazar, and leaning over, one to Sixto. As he handed the lemon plate, his hand brushed Sixto's almost unobtrusively. Sixto stared at Rik stonily. Balthazar looked down at his tea.

"Why," Rik asked brightly, "would the *Policía* be interested in me?"

"Routine," Balthazar replied. "We're looking into the background of John Haverford. He's a friend of Susan McKinley, one of the Strangler's victims. You indicated that you know Haverford."

"Oh yes, but you can't be thinking that Johnny. . . . Heavens, no!"

"Is Haverford a homosexual?"

"Well, now, that's a difficult question to answer, Officer. It is my firm belief that all men are attracted to their own sex. Some are thoroughly brainwashed while young, of course. Their very hostility to those of us who are honest and open about it merely illustrates the rightness of my belief. If they did not feel the powerful attraction, they would simply ignore us. Instead we are continually harassed. You can imagine what I would suffer if the navy knew. . . . I do appreciate the fact that that little contretemps the other day was *not* a matter of record."

"I'm curious about that incident. Given your career in the military, surely your action—"

"But who could have thought—that dreadful woman!" Rik interrupted excitedly. "Not I suppose *terribly* unattractive. *Nice* jewelry. She even looked the teeniest bit Joan Collins-y. But overweight. She'd have to lose at least twenty pounds. I had *no* idea how far her insane jealousy would drive her! And her husband—so good-looking—but one could see the man was entirely miserable. I thought that if ever a man needed to rethink his life! A few words from the right person, at the right time, he would simply . . . bloom."

He beamed at them, then sampled the tea. Balthazar noticed that Sixto had unconsciously hitched up his trouser leg slightly so that the gun was in full view through the glass table.

"I *was* naughty." Rik smoothed his robe carefully. "'Pricio is always telling me, and he would be so cross if he knew. But you see, in terms of my career, well, I am a radar expert. I get attractive re-enlistment bonuses, you know, as one of those with critical skills. 'Pricio, of course, is always imploring me to leave the service, and he certainly is doing very, very well himself. But one has one's pride. I can retire in just under ten years. And I'll only be thirty-eight. I enjoy—"

"About Haverford," Balthazar cut in. "Is he one of the brainwashed, or does he admit his true feelings?"

"Johnny—now that is sad. He won't even discuss it with me. I have tried. We wind-surf together, sometimes we sail, too. But the poor boy is, well, *was*, quite gone over La McKinley. And she, even with all his money, she simply would not—"

"Did you know Susan?"

"Not I. I never met her. But he talked about her a great deal."

"Did you know Imelda Torres?"

Janssen wrinkled his brow. It was, Balthazar suspected, a conscious movement.

"No, Officer, not to the absolute best of my knowledge. I've never even seen the woman. I did look carefully at her newspaper photographs, thinking I just might have seen her. I've read all about the case. So horrible."

"How about Karen Hoover, the baseball player?"

"No, and I *never* go to baseball games. I don't believe in spectator sports, you see. One should engage in athletics oneself. Quite silly to pay someone else to play tennis for you, don't you agree? A little more tea?"

"No, thank you," Balthazar replied. Sixto glared, stood up abruptly, and walked to the window.

"Could you give us an account of your whereabouts last Friday, Saturday, and Sunday evenings?" Balthazar asked patiently.

"Oh my. Am *I* a suspect? Let me see. Last Friday? I was at the Roof Resort, I'm sure. I always go there on Fridays when 'Pricio is out of town. A charming little bar in Old San Juan. It has a lovely view of the Customs House. An architectural jewel, isn't it? That lovely pink, with that gorgeous gold trim. And one can sit there in the open air and watch the cruise ships come in. They look like enormous birthday cakes on the horizon. And they have cunning little nooks where one can relax and—"

"What time did you arrive?"

"I should think I got there nine-ish."

"Could anyone verify that for us?"

"Well, there are these little nooks, and people aren't really looking around that much, you understand. . . ."

Sixto cleared his throat.

"Really, Officer," he looked beseechingly at Sixto, "don't get me flustered. I am trying . . . oh, yes. They had a live band on Friday. I danced a great deal. People would certainly have noticed. I rather think I danced the night away."

"How about Saturday?"

"Now, Saturday. I do have an alibi there! A quite good one. But I would just prefer that this doesn't get to 'Pricio. Of course, he knows that when he's gone. . . . But I'm sure Julian would vouch for me. Julian St. John. He's British. They pronounce that last name *Sinjun*. He lives in Old San Juan on San Sebastián Street. I was with him from late in the afternoon until Sunday morning. And now that I think, we strolled over to the Casablanca Café for an earlyish dinner. They know Julian. But Sunday night I just turned in early. I knew I was going to have a bear of a day on Monday."

"We will have to contact these people," Balthazar said, getting up. Sixto snapped his notebook shut.

Rik stood up. He towered over Sixto. "If ever—"

Sixto stalked across the room, yanked open the door, and turned to Rik. "If ever I hear that you asked a tourist for the time of day, I'll get you for soliciting. Be careful, Twinkle-feet."

Twinkle-*feet*? thought Balthazar, following Sixto out.

"Do call me Rik," Rik sang down the staircase.

It was later in the afternoon. Balthazar shoved the paperwork aside, rubbed his eyes, and looked at his watch. Sixto would be tied up the rest of the day in court.

The note from the Strangler had not changed his conviction that the man was not choosing victims at random, he thought wearily.

If the note really was from the Strangler. The panic in the city—the constant, but not necessarily unpleasant excitement—tilted the universe slightly for those already on the edge of sanity. Some of these unstable people might well be among the horde of sensation seekers, endlessly crossing the streets between headquarters and the arena parking lot. They were not the vacant-eyed street crazies, attracted by any gathering that gave them a chance to break up their monotonous days and find new trash cans to pick through. These people seemed normal enough, but events like this brought out hidden obsessions, fears, prejudices. If it were the police in the news, they often addressed their long complaining letters—or short, vituperative notes—to the particular officer shown in the papers or on TV. Their communications often had nothing to do with the particular case reported on—often they were concerned with the mismanagement of pet cemeteries, noisy motorcycles, illegal parking on residential streets, or even poor mail delivery.

But sometimes they wrote about the case. In the course of the River Rat investigation, the NYPD had received hundreds of crank letters. Although these people might be unbalanced, they could be clever. And they, too, might dislike

North Americans. As for the information in the letter, the writer might have overheard an unwary remark by an officer about the chokehold. It could happen.

But most of the other detectives Balthazar had talked to that day seemed satisfied that the note he had received was from the Strangler. And they were more sure now that the crimes were motiveless—the killer was fitting that part of the pattern more closely. And even policemen are influenced by what they read and hear. The media remained convinced that all women were threatened by a shadowy, vicious strangler who preyed upon solitary females. It made better copy. It involved the citizenry more immediately. It built indignation, nurtured fear and suspicion. Anyone could be the next victim. Anyone could be the unbalanced killer. Everyone bought newspapers, stayed tuned in for the latest word.

He had to admit that no evidence had turned up suggesting that the dead women knew each other. Karen Hoover had spent a great deal of time at the university gym, but McKinley didn't swim there, and Imelda Torres's aerobics classes were on the other side of the campus. Maybe the killer simply chose the area because there were large numbers of women.

And in several ways, this case conformed to the pattern of random killings. The women were robbed of life, stripped of their clothing, dumped. Someone was displaying his power over them, even though they were not molested. They were being treated as objects, disposable objects. Ted Bundy had told the police that he was surprised when he read about one of his victim's disappearance in the local papers. He had thought she was too inconsequential. Another killer had been amazed when a victim had fought back ferociously—as if a piece of furniture had refused to be turned into firewood.

In trying to catch the River Rat, the New York police, Balthazar included, had painstakingly checked on connections between the victims. Then he had never doubted, though, that the victims had no previous acquaintance with the killer. Now he was certain there was a link somewhere.

The time frame fit the idea of a killer with a motive. Usually there was more of a delay. . . . He had to take each girl's case in turn, comb their backgrounds very carefully. He would first concentrate on Susan McKinley. He hadn't talked to her parents yet. Perhaps she'd been a letter writer. They might know a lot about her friends and they might be more forthcoming, less suspicious of the police, than Maira Knight now.

Furthermore, he remembered smiling slightly, they were supposed to be staying with Mrs. Knight.

He could drive out there quickly, accomplish something. And this time he would rehearse carefully what he would say to her. This interview would go smoothly.

He took the elevator down to the police parking lot, was waved to the brown Nova by a harried dispatcher, and drove purposefully out into the January sunshine.

9

A S HE DROVE, he kept checking his rear and side mirrors. Pulling into the central business section with its gleaming bank towers and office buildings, he realized he was certainly being followed—by half the city. The rush hour started much earlier here than he had guessed.

How had the note writer located him so quickly? Following anybody in heavy traffic called for luck—and some practice. Didn't the bastard have to work?

But perhaps he hadn't needed to follow him to the hotel. Maybe he had a friend in the media—reporters could always find out. No effort had been made to conceal Balthazar's whereabouts. Or perhaps he even had a friend at headquarters who casually mentioned the name of Marten's hotel.

It could even be *from* someone at headquarters. Balthazar had been avoiding the thought. Yet it was a reasonable explanation, given the information in the note. His presence could be resented by others who disguised their hostility better than Negrón did. The note could be an attempt at intimidation. Helmsley had said that an outsider working with the San Juan police would certainly be eyed with suspicion. Some agents might wonder just what or who he was supposed to be investigating.

Worse, his presence could even be dangerous for someone on the police force. Could these deaths be linked to the Casera killing? Would anyone cold-bloodedly murder three other women to throw up a smokescreen for that crime? There was no indication that the dead women had suspected they were in danger. The three victims would not be suspicous of a policeman—uniformed or not. Further, it was clear that each of the killings had been engineered by a professional, just like Teresa Casera's murder.

Villareal would be the logical one to talk it over with. In the interview in his office that morning, the homicide chief had not been at all reassured by the idea that Balthazar was safe because he was surrounded by *Policía*. But even if he shared Balthazar's suspicions, what action would Villareal take? He did not know the man well enough to decide. Helmsley had said Captain Almon could be trusted. And Sixto, he thought, certainly. Tomorrow, it was a problem he would have to deal with.

He was walking up the pathway to Maira Knight's house before he quite realized it. He decided he would begin with an apology for disturbing her—vaguely worded to include his disastrous last visit as well. He would ask to talk to the McKinleys, but mention calmly that he would like to have a few words with her later. And he would avoid the subject of John Haverford.

She opened the door and regarded him in silence. He had the sudden, uncomfortable thought that she could read his mind. Wearing high heels, her eyes were almost level with his. Her lilac-colored blouse made her eyes seem lilac, too. Her hair, piled on her head and held with lavender combs, was escaping in small strands that curled around her neck.

He stammered slightly when asking to see Susan's parents.

".I expect them very soon," she said, without moving, "but they haven't come back yet. They did decide to stay here. I visited them at the Dupont when they arrived, and the hotel seemed so impersonal. . . ." She gave the impression of talking to give herself time to think, as if she were hesitant to ask him in.

A buzzer went off in the back of the house. "The chicken must be done. Just a moment—"

She turned, and he followed her in. The sight of her had so confused him that he almost had to remind his legs to move.

Ignoring him, she turned off the timer and lifted a heavy pan of simmering chicken that smelled lightly of onion off the stove, and put it in the sink. Then with a tongs she lifted out each piece and put it on a large wooden cutting board. "My mother was a fanatic about chicken," she said. "Her favorite refrain was, 'Keep it hot, keep it cold, or don't keep it.' Ever since, I hover over chicken like a hen."

She's talking to avoid silence, he thought. He didn't answer, but sat down on the edge of a high stool across from the sink. Rose had once told him that many very pretty women were shy, a problem made worse by the fact that they were stared at by strangers.

She opened the refrigerator and took out a bottle of Blanc De Blancs and put it by his elbow. She faced him at last.

"After you left, I was telling Paolo how furious I was, and then I realized I was being unreasonable. You have to investigate the girls' backgrounds. It was just that I was upset because I'd made that remark about John Haverford."

She gestured toward the wine. "I'm going to put some of this in the sauce. Would you like a glass?"

He nodded.

"I meant," she began again, "that, well, John is very bright—he reads omnivorously. And he's very good at all kinds of things. Susan said he'd fitted up the galley of his sailboat perfectly—cabinets and little drawers everywhere. But, with people, perhaps because he's embarrassed about the way he sounds, he just sits like a lump. I've always felt a little sorry for him. And I knew that Susan didn't want just a friend who shared her interests. Like all young girls, she was dreaming of romance."

There was a faint flush on her pale skin as she worked, perhaps from the heat of the range. The walls above the stove, the long counter, and the sink were covered half-way up with hand-painted orange and yellow tiles. Solid-colored tiles were intermixed with abstract drawings of fat orange suns, strutting ocher roosters, and lemon daisies with elongated petals. The pale yellow refrigerator looked relatively new but one side already showed signs of the ever-present tropical rust. A yellow phone hung on the wall next to Balthazar's stool.

"What are you making?" he asked.

"It's my nephew's favorite dish—*pollo al nido*—chicken in the nest. You cook the chicken with a sweet chili pepper and onion and bone it. Then you make a sauce with butter, milk, flour, wine, and some spices, and put the chicken in the sauce. The part Rico likes, though, is that you make little individual pastries or a nest of bread crumbs and heat it again. I promised to save him some. Lena took the boys to her parents. I thought it might be easier for the McKinleys if. . . ."

"Is Rico a sister's son?"

"Yes," she answered, her attention on making the sauce. "It's a long story. But it's worked out well for both of us."

"Were you married long before your husband was sent to Vietnam?"

"No, and I was always sure Mike would come back, that somehow it was a mistake. How could he be dead? One minute he was kissing me good-bye and cracking jokes. He's a real joker. Very large and very blond. We were married as soon as he finished pilot training. He was so young, and I was even younger. He'd only been a pilot a year, and he loves flying. He flew a Phantom, an F4C. His name is Michael D. Knight. They called him Captain Midnight."

He noticed how she wavered between past tense and present tense.

"So I started taking classes to fill up the time. Now I've finished my doctorate." She paused. "It's funny talking about Mike. Until Paolo showed up a few months ago, I hadn't talked about him for years. But Paolo was in Vietnam with him, and they were close. Maybe it has something to do with Paolo being adopted and not having a brother. Or probably it was that kind of war."

She lifted the chilled wine bottle from the ice bucket, and a drop of the water slid slowly down her arm like a tear. "Mike could still be alive, but in a prison camp? I don't even want to think about it. I feel like a widow, but not quite. You can't make plans for a new life."

He thought about how hard that was even when one was sure. He looked outside and noticed with surprise that it was twilight. In the winter, even in the tropics, the day ended abruptly. Somewhere in the yard a little coqui, the tiny tree frog, was carefully repeating his name: *ko kee*. No human voice could say it more clearly, he thought. The upward inflection at the end of the word made it seem as if the frog were wondering who he was.

The darkening air outside made the cheerful yellow of the kitchen more welcome. He thought of how often he had sat like this, wineglass in hand, watching Rose as she moved about their kitchen. She'd had a soft voice, like Maira's, with just an occasional short New York vowel. Why, he wondered, are we drawn to some members of the opposite sex, while others, although equally good-looking, don't stir the heart? Body language experts say that a stranger across a crowded room attracts a given person by movements alone. That could be true. Or maybe, he speculated, the scientists will discover that humans, although unaware of it, are enticed by an individual's scent.

"Was Susan especially attracted to any other men?" he asked.

"She seemed to like older ones. That's what made me think of the romance business. For a long time, she was infatuated with one of her professors. And lately she seemed to be making up excuses to drop by when she knew Paolo might be here. I don't think he even noticed her," she finished sadly.

"How did you feel about Susan?"

She put the ladle on a spoon rest, and leaning against the stove, gazed directly into his eyes. "I cared a. . . ." she began, then stopped abruptly. "I notice your skeptical eyebrow, Lieutenant."

She turned back to the stove. "You mean did I resent her intrusion? Look, Paolo is only a. . . ." Her tone suddenly became dry. "This conversation is really about me, isn't it? A subtle grilling? For a moment there, I thought you were being understanding."

"Please," Balthazar began, "I wanted you to—"

The wall phone next to his ear rang. She reached over, picked up the receiver, then handed it to him wordlessly.

"I'm really sorry," he said distractedly. "I had to give a phone number." She didn't reply.

The dispatcher's clipped voice asked him to turn on his car radio immediately. He moved toward the front hall. "Look, I'll have to check the car radio," he said, "but—"

"You needn't bother waiting any longer, Lieutenant," she said coolly. "I'll have the McKinleys call when they arrive."

Balthazar climbed into the car and clicked the radio on in a white fury. She'd really misinterpreted his words, his expression. It was that damned scar above his eyebrow. Why was she so damn prickly? Maira Knight was an impossible, intriguing woman.

The operator gave him the information in an expressionless voice. Another body, near the university, another woman strangled. He told her he was near there and asked for directions.

He did not notice that, as he sped off, another car pulled out of a space down the street, its headlights dark, and followed him.

10

THE STREETS WERE almost deserted as Balthazar raced toward the campus. In the Condado area, the casinos stay open until the early morning hours, and tourists stroll through the warm, brilliantly lit streets. But here in the Río Piedras section of San Juan, as on the rest of the island, people went to bed as it grew dark. Only a few people clustered in the soft orange glow of the street lights in the small gardens by a handsome church.

He turned into the gates of the spacious main campus of the University of Puerto Rico. Like many universities, UPR had grown quickly, but the modern structures did not seem to jostle the older buildings or the dignified old tower. During the day, the area was alive with students hurrying or strolling down the walks landscaped attractively with the flowers and plants native to the island. Now only a line of cars, headed like his own to the murder scene, disturbed its sleepy peace.

The university layout was confusing, partly because of the growth, partly because the signs, if there were signs at all, merely laconically stated the names of the buildings, not their functions. Barriers appeared out of nowhere, directing one to park elsewhere. But the dispatcher's directions were good, and as he drove down the narrow lane to the faculty parking lot, Balthazar could see where the body must be. Normally, it was a dark field just beyond the lot. Now it was as brightly lit as a stage. A section was roped off and floodlights were trained on it. In addition, there were the quick, brilliant flashes of the police photographers' cameras and, all around the cordon, the blinding lights of the television camera crews.

As Balthazar walked into the light, the reporters, confined to the edges of the area, began to shout at him in English and Spanish. He shook his head at the barrage of queries and joined Villareal, who stood staring mournfully at a covered bundle. The chief leaned down and jerked back the sheet. A woman's naked body lay sprawled gracelessly on the grass.

She was lying on her stomach, face twisted to her right. She was older than the previous victims. Her thick black hair, bunched over her left shoulder, had strands of gray that turned to silver in the artificial light. Her rounded hips and heavy thighs had the look of approaching middle age.

The medical examiner had already done her work, but was still standing in the shadows, holding her kit. She was shaking her head firmly as she spoke with the district attorney, who gestured animatedly.

Balthazar looked carefully at the body. The nude back was splotched with small dark bruises, and there was a faint line around the back of the neck. Curtly, Villareal ordered the men to turn her over onto her back. Her large breasts flopped clumsily to the sides of her body as they moved her.

She had been a handsome woman once, Balthazar thought, standing back as Villareal bent over, peering at her throat. Now she looked lumpish, eyes staring emptily at the sky. But when the energy of life had filled the body, making the dark eyes snap, the breasts lift . . . but the energy was gone.

Villareal beckoned him forward, pointing to the mark across the front of the woman's neck. Ugly purplish marks were scattered on her arms and her torso. On the top of her left thigh, there was a huge bruise.

"Made by the killer's knee?" Balthazar asked.

"It is certain it is not his usual method." Fatigue made Villareal's voice raspy. "I wanted you to see this at the scene. Perhaps he was unlucky this time." He considered. "She wriggled out of his armlock and he had to push her against something, grab a necklace from the back and pull?"

"But then there wouldn't be any marks on the *back* of her neck. Supposing he knocks her down, straddles her. He could have used the lapel chokehold. Crossed two pieces of her blouse or dress and twisted."

"Yes, or . . . we have here someone who is thinking to fool us. To imitate the Strangler. He has killed in a rage, but then he thinks. He takes off her clothing and puts her near the campus. A copycat killer. She was not killed here—almost no sign of a struggle. She probably was not even undressed here. You notice her broken fingernails. If it has happened as you describe, she will have marked him. We would be lucky if it were the Strangler." He sounded pessimistic.

"The doctor able to say anything helpful yet?"

"She says only that the woman has been dead some hours. Rigor mortis has already come and gone. We do not yet know who the victim is."

Villareal inhaled deeply and blew the air quietly through his nose. "I will tell the reporters we will have a conference for them later. Much, much later. But perhaps early this morning."

"Was it him? Did he do it? Strangler's work?" The newsmen on the edges of the crowded area yelled the insistent question at any of the detectives near them. The video cameras scanned, the photographers clicked, their flashbulbs like fireflies. Ignoring the media, some of the agents searched the clipped grass near the outer edges of the roped-off section; others were making notes. The ambulance attendants unloaded the stretcher and stood, joking with one another, waiting for permission to remove the corpse. Balthazar noticed Negrón standing with folded arms, watching the activity, chewing on a toothpick. He avoided Balthazar's glance.

"Where is Cardenas?" Villareal asked suddenly.

"I was near here. I came alone," Balthazar said briefly.

Villareal's eyes flicked over his face, then back to the body, still obscenely illuminated by the harsh lights. "I am going back—come in my car. We can discuss what information to release. The Secretary of Justice will no doubt be at headquarters. He will want to speak with you about this. He will be thinking of the journalists who will be preparing for the morning's papers and newscasts. Alvalos," he beckoned to the round-faced young officer. "Take the lieutenant's keys, and bring his car to the station."

The agent scooped up the keys with a grin, and Balthazar explained where the car was parked.

But Villareal seemed in no hurry to move. He straightened his mustache carefully with his fingers, watching the ambulance back up to the ropes, the men walking toward the body. "If this is not the Strangler's work, everyone must be told this at once. So we will concentrate on that. But I have something to—"

"Lieutenant, Lieutenant, you've forgotten your notebook."

Balthazar turned and saw Alvalos hurrying back toward the lighted area, a black clipboard notebook held out at arm's length. He waved it, his youthful face reflecting his pleasure in being helpful.

The flash of light from the notebook's explosion was brighter than the television lights. Alvalos's body was hurled backward and lay still, his arms flung out on the grass like a broken doll's. Around him, people dropped to the ground, and then almost immediately scrambled up again. The noise was still echoing in their ears, and they were all running toward the young man in silence.

"I am most relieved that you are uninjured, Lieutenant Marten."

Although it was five o'clock in the morning, Secretary of Justice Cortes wore an elaborately embroidered long-sleeved shirt and looked as if he had just showered and shaved. He looked, in fact, as if he were ready to face the hot lights of the television crew and make an announcement which would dominate that day's headlines. Which is exactly what he was preparing to do. His smile only touched his lips.

He went on meditatively, "We were all fortunate, in a sense. Even poor young Alvalos. He has lost most of his forearm, but if he had jiggled the notebook as he slipped it out from under the car seat, he would probably have lost his life. That kind of explosive is more effective against a firm base, I am told. Initial reports indicate that it was probably a Claymore mine—very popular during the Vietnam War. Not that difficult to make, BBs pressed on a flat sheet of gelignite. We'll know for certain after the fragment analysis. And the fact that Alvalos was not near anyone else at the time was extremely lucky. The wounds suffered by others bled a lot, but they were superficial."

He cleared his throat and looked at Balthazar. Balthazar was sure of the next topic of discussion.

Back to New York.

He had thought about it. First, like a slowly unwinding nightmare, he had gone over in his mind the drive to Maira Knight's house. He had been concentrating on the unfamiliar streets and the rush-hour traffic. From her house to the campus, he had been preoccupied with the thought of a fourth murder. He simply had not glanced down, had not noticed a notebook. It was the type he'd been using: two plastic sides that folded over an inside pad, which held by a metal clip.

He had been asked repeatedly. It could have been in the car all the time, or slipped in later, even at the murder scene. He could not tell them.

It was under the passenger seat, they said. The metal clasp at the top would have stuck out slightly. If he had not been driving, if he had climbed in as he usually did, he would surely have stepped on it. He had thought about that.

Or if he had leaned over from the driver's side, tried to pull it out. He had imagined it. A fierce, gnawing anger had pushed away the fear that had made his stomach jump. A rat-toothed anger that did not go away. He did not want to go back to New York now.

They seemed determined to send him there.

"I am responsible for your safety, Lieutenant, because I initiated your assignment." The Secretary spoke quickly as if to forestall any interruption. "The *Superintendente*, Chief Villareal, we all agree. This lunatic, for whatever reason, has focused his hostility on you personally. There can no longer be any doubt. But we feel that if you were reassigned in New York, he would probably not pursue his . . . vendetta. Therefore, we have reserved a seat for you on a flight—"

"I understand your position, Sir." Balthazar fought to keep his voice dispassionate. "*And* I appreciate your concern. But I'm asking you to reconsider. I have no idea what I can do to solve this case, or that I would be any more useful than the next man. But clearly the Strangler—or someone—believes I'm a threat. And we should—*I* should—be given a chance to discover why he thinks so. I can't do that in New York."

"Perhaps. But the psychiatrists who examined his note to you are in some agreement on one point. The man is hurling obscenities at you because he has been made to feel inferior in some way by men like you. Policemen, possibly. If he is Puerto Rican, he may resent you simply because you are from the United States. He mentions in the note specifically that you are a New Yorker. You understand that some Puerto Ricans are ambivalent about our countries' relationship. We are not a state, but we have been citizens since 1917. We use your currency, serve in your military, and there are no trade barriers. We all recognize the benefits of our association, but some also resent those very benefits."

Balthazar leaned forward, started to interrupt again. The Secretary held up his hand. "Wait. The doctors think the man is so intent on proving that he is as 'good' as you that he will persist in his efforts to outdo you. In other words, to kill you."

"Assuming the note is from the Strangler, what explanation do they give for the fact that although he is competing with me, his targets so far have been women?"

"They have an explanation." A wry smile twisted the Secretary's face. "Psychiatrists always do. They say that one of his expressions, 'as useless as three tits,' subtly indicates his dismissal of women. Not necessarily contempt for the sex, Lieutenant, but a conviction that females do not matter. He can kill them without compunction. But these women are valuable to some men. Only men are important to him. Hence his feeling that he is triumphing over a *man*. You represent the kind of male adversary he wishes to best."

"But don't you agree, Sir, that is only one possible explanation for his behavior? Suppose, instead, that he is a man with a motive for killing at least one of these particular women. He may know that is the angle I am pursuing. He may fear what I will discover."

The Secretary looked at Balthazar sharply. "Do you really believe that the Strangler is not a madman?"

"It's at least a strong possibility. He says in his note that he *is* crazy. Yet even the most lunatic insist they are sane."

"The doctors mentioned that also, but they were divided on the significance of the remark. He says, 'Even crazy I am good.' He could have meant, 'Even if I were crazy, I am good at what I do.' Killing is what he does. And, how does the man know what aspect of the case you are investigating? We have not told the media that you are looking for a motive."

"There's other evidence that he has information, or at least a source of information."

Balthazar stared unhappily over the Secretary's shoulder. "But the kind of thing he knows—my hotel, what I'm working on—could have been mentioned in many kinds of conversations. It means nothing. What I want to stress is that it could be essential to find out why the Strangler perceives me as a threat."

The Secretary frowned, pursed his lips. "There are real advantages for us in having your help. But in staying here you are endangering your own life. It is essential to remember that, too, Lieutenant."

"I want to stay," Balthazar said.

"We could at least release a report saying that you are no longer working on this case."

"You don't want to do that, Sir, I'm sure. Nor do I want you to."

The Secretary rose. "Very well," he said. "We are grateful, Lieutenant."

He opened the door to his office and turned, hand on the doorknob. "Perhaps the public will be calmed knowing that the Strangler is now attacking the police, instead of our citizens."

11

A CLEAN SHIRT AND a shave. Balthazar walked down the corridor thinking that at the moment that's what he needed, at the very least. Villareal would know where his suitcase had been taken, but the chief was at the press conference. He slumped wearily down in a chair. It'd been the longest five days of his life. Nothing was routine—everything was new. And just when he had to think clearly, he'd been tossed by foaming breakers of emotions. He rested his head back against the wall. If he waited until the Secretary was on camera, he might be able to leave the building unnoticed by the reporters and the crowd.

Here at the Special Investigations Bureau in Puerta de Tierra, as at Police Headquarters in a different section of San Juan, citizens and media people congregated noisily outside. Elected officials, who were more amenable to interviews, gathered here. It was difficult to enter or leave without being stopped. Some of the people waiting outside were anxious parents of missing girls who now feared that their daughters were early victims of the Strangler. Others were simply frightened and seeking reassurance. Some were the usual curiosity seekers. Some wanted to be on camera.

If there were no officials to talk to, the reporters diligently conducted man-on-the-street interviews. Public reactions covered a wide range. Indignation that God and the police, not necessarily in that order, allowed this to happen. Whispered prayers for the poor tormented soul of the killer. Shouted curses. Quite a few of the interviewees had suggestions for catching the man. More than a few insisted that they knew who he was. Two had even confessed to the killings.

Balthazar found it difficult to face their storm of questions, comments, fears. How did politicians do it, he wondered. The crowd's hysteria seemed to press on his skin with a physical force.

People's emotions. He thought of the psychiatrists' impression that the Strangler felt women were inconsequential. He would have to ask them if they thought that was the reaction of a homosexual. He'd always imagined that homosexuals *envied* women. Perhaps the Strangler was asexual.

He remembered reading interviews with Henry Lee Lucas, who at one point claimed he'd killed 360 people. Even if many police departments were trying to dump their "losers," their unsolved cases, on Lucas's head, even if Lucas were fantasizing, attention seeking, he surely had killed one—his mother.

Lucas described his mother as brutal, constantly beating him, bringing home men and having sex with them in front of him. He claimed to have no sexual desire, admitted to having relations with his homosexual traveling partner, but said he didn't enjoy it.

Balthazar believed that. In answering the interviewer's direct questions, Lucas could not bring himself to use words, even the simplest, to describe the sex act. Not acceptable words, not unacceptable words. He tried to avoid questions about his sexual feelings. He much preferred to talk about his killings.

And Lucas varied his method. He claimed to have murdered his victims in every way possible. "I even filleted them like a fish," he had said at his trial.

It is necessary to have known love to feel it.

He recalled the vaguely silly simper he'd seen on the faces of Lucas, of the Son of Sam, after they'd been captured. His instinct said they would not see that expression on the face of the Strangler. This man would stare contemptuously at the cameras. In fact, he could see Angel Negrón doing just that.

Balthazar thought of the anxious fear he had detected in Villareal's eyes, the grim suspicion in those of the Secretary of Justice. They were afraid that the Strangler might be one of them.

A compelling case could be made for the fear, the suspicion. If a skillful defense attorney, by insinuating that the mysterious Strangler might also have killed Teresa Casera, won the day, charges against the two officers would be dropped. Because of the Casera case, the Bureau of Special Investigations, a branch of the Justice Department, received permission to launch a full-scale investigation of the *Policía*. If the officers were found innocent, there would be no investigation.

More than one police officer might be relieved.

Such men would have a particular reason for forcing him off the case. Many would have military backgrounds. Some had served in Korea, some in Vietnam. All had complete access to any information.

Any one of them, even if he were not involved in the murders, could have written the note, just to get rid of an outsider. It was even possible, he thought bleakly, that there was a conspiracy. If that were true, Police Headquarters was the most dangerous place for him to be.

He jerked when a large hand tapped him on the shoulder.

Swinging around, he turned and saw Montez.

"I can take you back for a change of clothing."

Balthazar stood up, eyed the man's enormous bulk, and hesitated.

"We must check with the dispatcher," Montez said expressionlessly. "We'll leave our location."

"It would be best to eat first," the big man said as they reached the car. "There is an all-night, open-air café in Santurce. The food is very good there."

As they drove through the quiet streets, he looked closely at Balthazar's pale, drawn face as if to diagnose an illness. "You need eggs," he grunted. "At this place, the eggs are perfect. They do not cook them too quickly, getting the edges brown and hard.

"But," he continued ruminatively, "perhaps a nice *hamburguesa*. *Grande*, not one of those thin little slices of meat that a cow would not recognize. They do proper ones. Just cooked, pink in the middle, juicy. And good *papas fritas*, too. Crisp outside, soft in the middle."

Balthazar, who had been thinking he was more tired than hungry, began to think he was more hungry than tired.

As they ate, Balthazar began to feel better. He would talk to Captain Almon before full-scale paranoia set in. He liked Montez. Although it made no sense, he couldn't imagine anyone who ate that heartily being a conspirator.

Then again, all Puerto Ricans were serious about food. Every highway was lined with food vendors. Roadside stands with fresh-baked bread still warm from the oven, peddlers on every median with fruit. People setting up portable generators to heat the grills to barbecue chicken, turn rotisseries, or to run the blenders mixing the pineapple juice with the heavy, rich coconut milk. Building fires to cook the pigs, then slowly turning them on spits.

He mentioned this to Montez. "At any given moment half of this island is cooking for the other half."

"And why not?" Montez answered placidly, taking a huge bite out of his hamburger. He chewed fastidiously. "The best food, however, is cooked in one's home. My wife, Teresa, usually on Sundays, makes a big pot of *mondongo*." He described precisely how this was done. The tripe and calf's feet would be rubbed with limes and simmered for a long time. Then Teresa would add ham, pumpkin, root vegetables, garbanzo beans, onions, peppers, garlic, fresh cilantro leaves, and tomato sauce. The smell would fill the house and tickle the taste buds. He added, "My daughter Angelita is also a very good cook. *And* she has a good batting average. However, Rosarita's pitching has made her team the fifth best on the island."

"You have two daughters?" Balthazar was a little confused at the change of subject.

"Four. Carmencita is a utility infielder, and Matilde plays first base. My brother-in-law Luis has four sons who only like to fix cars." He took the last bite of his hamburger with every sign of satisfaction.

When he'd at last pushed his plate back, he turned to Balthazar. "I have heard. This woman tonight—we are turning the case over to Homicide Two. There is a good suspect."

"She has been identified?"

"Her sister reported her missing. The sister says the woman's lover, a house painter, was often drunk and abusive. He will have scratches on him. Homicide Two will find him." Montez shrugged and lapsed into silence.

Finally he roused himself again. "We have not been completely open with you, Lieutenant. Now we regret this very much. But from the beginning, Chief Villareal and I have been looking into the question of a suspect on our own force. We had only vague suspicion. Now, we have discussed this with Captain Almon. He has urged us to continue, of course, especially. . . . You understand that we had no evidence. We *have* no evidence. After much searching, none. Negrón—and I mention his name as a mere example—is able to account for his whereabouts. And you understand that it is much, much better if this remains confidential. You will, of course, want to have a word with the Captain. I must also tell you that I have met with *El Vampiro*."

"Ah, yes," Balthazar said, remembering Villareal's praise of Montez's best "source." "Why the name? Does he look like a bat?"

"*Mira*, I had not thought of that. And there is just a little point to the top of the ear, too. . . . But he himself chose that name to communicate with me. He moves silently and hears everything."

"A street person?"

"No, no. He is a man *muy importante*. He is a man of many affairs, none of them in the limits of the law. He would not sell information to the *Policía*. Once I did a favor for his family. Still, in most circumstances, he would say nothing. This is different. The man himself has a young daughter," he concluded, as if that would explain all.

Montez ran his hand over his large mustache. "Of course, it is fortunate that I spoke to him before Alvalos was injured. *El Vampiro* might well feel some . . . sympathy for that action." He grimaced.

Balthazar waited and then asked, "Has he found out anything useful?"

"A man was seen leaving the car of the Torres girl, back behind the bar where it was finally found today. But the description was not at all good, and, you know, the car was stripped later. Tires, battery, stereo—all gone. Fingerprints everywhere, but who is to know whose? A thief who brought it there to take the parts where he would not be seen? The killer's? Those of later thieves? Bah!"

"Who saw the man?"

"A young boy. He waits outside the back entrance of the bar at night. It is . . . his job. This bar has dancers. If men leave unaccompanied, the boy asks them if they would like to meet these girls—or others. He is too young to arrest."

Montez belched softly. "But the lot is badly lit. And the car was parked in back, near some bushes. The boy waited for the man to come up to the back entrance. When he did not, he went back to see if by chance the man was drunk, had passed out, perhaps left the car unlocked. He only saw him from the back, hurrying off. But he did not pursue him. He had the impression that the man was a police officer."

"Why?"

"Who knows? He said only that he was tall and it was the way he walked. With a straight back."

"Was it perhaps what the man was wearing? A uniform?"

"The boy said there was very little light. He could not tell what the man had on."

"How tall was the man? Much over six feet?"

"The boy would have mentioned someone extremely tall."

"Could we talk to him?"

Montez stood up. "That is not possible, but it is not necessary. *El Vampiro* can question him in ways we could not, and besides the boy would tell him everything, hiding nothing. *El Vampiro* is now looking for those who stripped the car, but even he will find that hard. Besides the professional car parts thieves, we have many, many amateurs."

12

SIXTO WAS IN the fingerprint division down the hall, going over the reports on the innumerable smudged partials lifted from Imelda Torres's car. Balthazar sat at a desk in one of the partitioned areas in the Homicide Section. He was staring at the institutional beige wall, calculating that in the five days since he'd arrived, he'd had sixteen hours of sleep.

A gecko darted swiftly across the wall next to Balthazar's chair, but stopped abruptly when he leaned over to peer at it. The little house lizards had adapted nicely to life with man. They kept down the troublesome insects, and they were no problem themselves. The intricate brown and green patterns of their skins, so perfect as camouflage against the stems of the tropical plants and trees, were useless on these monotone walls. But still they froze if someone approached, pretending they were invisible. They even seemed to get a noncommittal look on their faces as they waited, hoping no one would notice them.

The lizard sped to the ceiling as Balthazar reached to answer the phone. A visitor was waiting for him in the conference room on the tenth floor.

A very short, trim, gray-haired man put aside the papers he had spread on the table next to a briefcase and rose to shake Balthazar's hand.

"Hornby Atwill," he said. "I hold the Bates Chair of Language." Each word was enunciated with loving precision. "I've been studying the note you received, Lieutenant. I've just finished, and I came right over. I would call the text revealing. I think I can safely say that."

He sat down and pointed to the first sheet of paper. On it was typed the first sentence of the note: YOU ARE A COCK-SUCKING MFER NEW YORKER WHO DOESN'T KNOW HOG SHIT.

The rest of the sheet of paper was filled with notations, in minute handwriting. Interspersed with the notes were what looked to Balthazar like abstruse mathematical symbols or hieroglyphics.

"The man is not a careful writer," Atwill said severely. "I can point to a number of obvious indications. He does not use commas, and he uses 'your' in the second sentence when he means 'you are.'"

"I can see that." Balthazar found himself amused by the little man's meticulous speech.

"Now I use the masculine pronoun primarily as a convenience, Lieutenant. But if the writer is a woman, she has served in the armed forces, and she is masculine in her . . . orientation. Concentrating on this first sentence, I find it most interesting that he does not write out the word *motherfucker*. And, of course, he is using the incorrect form."

Balthazar stared at him. "There's a *correct*—?"

"I mean, naturally, that he ought to have used the adjectival form, *motherfucking*. Since we can assume that, given the rest of the note, he does not abbreviate it lest he *offend* you, it gives us an indication of his age."

Balthazar looked at the sentence again. "How does this indicate his age?"

"Let me hasten to say, by itself, it is slender evidence. There are more solid hints. Heavens, 'solid hint'—an oxymoron. Now, the term *motherfucker* gained some general usage in the middle sixties. For those Americans born after that period, the term has lost a great deal of its original force. But for those born before that period, even those who habitually use taboo words, men who have spent some time in the military and in Vietnam, like this writer, there may be a certain hesitancy in *writing* the word out. The term might, for them, still create a mental picture. Now the expression 'doesn't know hog shit,' is of fairly recent vintage and, although the choice of *hog* shit—"

"Professor," Balthazar said, leaning back, "I would find it easier if you just gave me your conclusions."

"Well," Atwill looked doubtful, "you would have every right to be very uneasy about their correctness. Some of my conclusions are really inspired guesses. Others are more firmly based. But with slang, you must be prepared to venture. By the time most expressions find their way into a text, they are outmoded." Atwill's eyes shone with enthusiasm. "Now here in Puerto Rico we have an interesting phenomenon. I refer to it as 'ossified slang,' and I have written several articles on the subject for language journals. You see, many Puerto Ricans spend a period of their lives on the mainland where they learn current English expressions. Then they return here and speak Spanish almost exclusively. When they have occasion to speak English, they still use those outdated slang forms."

"Ah, Professor—" Balthazar looked at him in dismay.

"But everywhere some expressions have staying power in the spoken language, even if you cannot point to an incidence in print. Consider the sentence 'Blow it out yours asshole.' There should, of course, be a comma after 'yours.' That expression goes back to World War II. It is, however, still heard. And it is amusing that he first uses the abbreviated, and hence more polite, 'yours,' but then adds the understood taboo word 'asshole,' anyway." Atwill beamed.

"Please, Professor," Balthazar said.

"Very well. As I said, the text indicates to me that the man served in the military during the late 1960s, or early 1970s. That would give us his age in itself. He is over thirty. He served on the front lines rather than in some clerical capacity."

"His choice of language tells you that?"

"It's an inference, Lieutenant. I myself was a company clerk in the Korean War. One had to be able to punctuate, spell, type. This man is by no means illiterate, but he has a weak command of grammar."

An unexpected gleam of amusement glimmered in Atwill's eyes. "There were definite advantages to being company clerk. When I was bored with a place, or found it dangerous, I filled out the proper forms and reassigned myself."

He shuffled through his papers. "But, to continue. The writer has finished high school. He was raised in the United States, in the Southwest. I think Oklahoma, but northern Texas is an outside possibility."

"Oklahoma? But . . . could he be Hispanic?"

"He might well belong to that ethnic group, Lieutenant. But English was his first language."

"Would he have had to be *raised* in the Southwest? Suppose that he was merely stationed there in the military?"

"Very unlikely. Let me explain. Look at these two sentences: 'Tell them you want off' and 'I can blow you away with a bean shooter at a click.' The expression 'want off' originated in the Southwest but it is now in general American usage. But he uses the term *bean shooter*."

"As a child in New York, I had a pea shooter," Balthazar said. "So did all my friends. It was a sort of straw and you blew dried peas out of it."

"Would you ever refer to that boy's weapon as a 'bean shooter'?"

"No, I suppose not, simply because peas are round and fit in the straw."

"As a matter of fact, the term 'bean shooter' was used to mean a slingshot, a more lethal weapon, as Goliath discovered. It makes much more sense in the context of the sentence. He is using hyperbole, of course, since it would hardly be accurate at the distance of a kilometer. The point is that the term was used to indicate a slingshot in a very small geographical area of the Southwest and in pockets of the South. I would argue that is not the kind of term an adult would pick up, remember, and use in these circumstances. But it would seem quite natural to a writer who had heard it in his youth."

"Still, someone who was writing quickly, perhaps someone who spoke English as a child, but then recently has spoken far more Spanish, might use that term?"

"There are always many, many variables." Atwill sighed. "But this is a more exact science than you might think."

There was a quiet knock on the door, and Stan, the young agent, opened it. She'd had her hair cut recently, and it curled around her pretty face softly. "I'm sorry to disturb you, Lieutenant, but Chief Villareal would like to speak with you in his office as soon as possible."

Atwill looked at his papers in some disappointment. "I will provide a written report, detailing my arguments and giving the rest of my conclusions."

"Thank you, Professor. One quick question. Could this note have been written by someone whose knowledge of language was as thorough as yours?"

"Few people have as *thorough* a knowledge," Atwill began stiffly, but then he smiled broadly. "You mean, was this note written by a highly educated man who is endeavoring to imitate the style of a less educated one? A professor, perhaps? Several of my reactionary colleagues would prefer that women be banished from the university, but killing them one by one seems extreme. Nor do I think that they could act with quickness or resourcefulness. But there is a certain childlike bravado evidenced in this note that makes me think of professors I know. To answer your question, Lieutenant, it is in the realm of possibility."

Villareal was smiling, too. A thin smile, but given that his expressions had been ranging from dejection to depression recently, it passed for a sign of hilarious delight. He was waving some sheets of paper before a clearly baffled Sixto as Balthazar entered.

"You see what I have here? A report from the Institute of Forensic Medicine on Imelda Torres. And it is good news—a breakthrough at last. It seems that her body was not put in a freezer as was first thought. Not at all. She had been placed on Friday in a hyperbaric chamber!"

"A hyperbaric chamber?"

Villareal was so excited that the words tumbled out. "It has many, many uses. *Por ejemplo*, for the deep-sea divers. So they do not get, you know, the bends, the sickness from coming back too quickly to air with normal pressure and oxygen. One goes into this tubelike affair and the air pressure is changed, slowly, slowly until it is like the outside air."

He tapped the report triumphantly. "And, if you add even more oxygen, certain bacteria will not grow. Those bacteria that cause a body to decay then, you see, do not live. So the body is preserved much better. The pathologists conferred with Dr. Reiquam, an expert on cancer cells. He confirms that it would fit the conditions they observed in the woman's body."

"Does the university have a hyperbaric chamber?" Balthazar asked.

"We start with the one at the university. We are already talking to the head of the Oceanography Department there. He is getting the lists of people who would know how to use the chamber. We may have to wait until everyone can be found."

Villareal pursed his lips. "It is very early, and a weekend. Few people will be coming to the campus. And this professor says there are a number of possibilities—graduate students, as well as faculty. Even the janitorial staff must be checked. But now, at last, we can move forward. Our routine, working like the oiled watch, will narrow down these lists."

"We *start* with the one at the university? There's more than one?"

"Yes. These chambers are also used in medicine. The navy base at Roosevelt Roads has two. A very large one—called a 'multiplace' one—that doctors can go into with patients. They put a mask, like a pilot's, on the patient. This is the better kind. The patient does not get—" he looked at his notes, "—confinement anxiety. The other kind, the 'monoplace,' is like a large cylinder, and the whole body is placed in that. It bothers the very sick to be shut up, to be so confined. It is not much bigger than a coffin. The navy uses their smaller one at the Naval Station for decompression, and as a backup in emergency cases when the larger one is in use."

"They would then be in use much of the time. Could a body be left there for several days?"

"At the base, they said it would not be possible in the big chamber. Occasionally the smaller one at the San Juan Naval Station is not used over the weekend. Our killer could not count on that. But it seems even more possible at the university's monoplace chamber. The doctors at the medical school use the navy's big one for critical cases. The small one at the Oceanography Department is used mostly for research. These chambers, they are expensive, you see. But when one is needed, for cases of carbon monoxide poisoning, for example, it is needed immediately."

"Can these chambers be operated by a man working alone?"

"So they say," Villareal replied. "Or so I *think* they say. They insist on long explanations. One man sounds doubtful and he makes it sound very difficult. The next says, 'Yes, but . . . .' The third says, 'Probably.' Still, the chances of finding traces, even part of a fingerprint . . . ."

Balthazar understood Villareal's relief. The Strangler was sounding like a stranger, not one of them, not a member of the *Policía*.

He explained the professor's theories about the author of the note left at the Dupont Plaza.

"His speculations, Lieutenant, will be helpful. Once we have a list of people with access to the chamber, we can inquire also about the place of upbringing. An additional factor. We have a breakthrough at last!"

On their way to Maira Knight's home to interview Susan McKinley's parents, Sixto checked the car mirrors more frequently than an armored truck driver with a factory payroll. The car had been meticulously searched before they were allowed to leave the police parking lot. All of the anxious care was making Balthazar nervous. At least, he thought, Maira Knight was unlikely to be present for the interview.

As they drew up to the house, the front door exploded open, and two small boys raced down the front walk, carrying light plastic baseball bats. Flipping a bright orange ball in the air, the marine sergeant, Paolo Davenport, followed them. The boys sped down the street, and he hurried after them, laughingly calling to them to slow down.

A plump young Puerto Rican woman with a shy smile met them at the still open screen door. She nodded when they introduced themselves, murmured that her name was Lena, and gracefully ushered them into the living room.

The McKinleys sat next to each other on the wicker couch with pale blue cushions. The husband rose and shook hands briskly. His short hair, his carefully trimmed small mustache, and his bearing all proclaimed the retired military man.

"Ray McKinley," he said in a booming voice that he quickly modulated. "And this is my wife Lois."

Mrs. McKinley was a pleasant-faced woman with faded blonde hair. Her gray eyes were blurred with tears that did not fall.

Across from them, sitting as if poised to spring at an improperly phrased question, was an unsmiling Maira Knight.

In Mrs. McKinley's lap were neatly wrapped packages of pale yellow envelopes. She gestured at them.

"They asked me to send for the letters that Susan wrote to us at home. She wrote every week, you know, quite faithfully. They only arrived this morning, so I haven't had a chance to glance over them. But, in any case, I don't think I'd. . . ."

She handed them to Balthazar. "We'd like them back, of course," she added softly.

He glanced down at the rounded, almost childish handwriting. "I'll certainly see that they're returned, Mrs. McKinley. Did Susan often mention her friends in her letters?"

"Yes, at least in passing. She'd list her activities during the week, you know, and talk about which friend she'd gone with to various functions. You could tell when she'd met a new young man—lots of exclamation points after his name. And she wrote so much about Maira and the boys and how much she enjoyed coming here."

She tried to smile at Maira, but the smile wobbled and then slipped. "We'd met some of her friends, of course. Johnny Haverford, naturally. She wrote a lot about him because she worried about him, I mean his lack of purpose in life."

Her husband, glancing at Balthazar as if he'd understand perfectly, said, "Nothing wrong with that boy a tour in the marines wouldn't have fixed. Even the navy. Probably still not too late."

"Now, Ray," his wife interjected, "he'll settle down. He's only five or six years older than. . . ." She faltered, looking down at her lap in anguish.

"Mrs. McKinley, did Susan ever mention any of John Haverford's friends?"

"Well, now, she did. She thought most of them were a bad influence on him and were taking advantage of his having all that money. I can't remember their names, but you'll see when you read the letters."

"Do you know where Haverford grew up?"

"Texas?" Mrs. McKinley said doubtfully, glancing at her husband, who shrugged. "Or do I just think that because Susan said something about his money coming from oil?"

Balthazar patiently drew out the couple, but they could add nothing. "Understand perfectly. You have to ask these questions. Part of the job. Need to be thorough," Ray McKinley said. But he was convinced, as was his wife, that their daughter's death was the result of an unfortunate chance encounter. "Probably driving by that damned beach and she just stopped on the spur of the moment," the colonel explained, the gruffness of his voice failing to conceal his pain.

As they left, Mrs. McKinley patted Balthazar's hand and murmured how relieved they were to have such a man on the case. Maira Knight was not smiling.

When they returned to headquarters, Balthazar was immediately called to the phone. He heard MacAtee's voice, sounding querulous.

"Your location some sort of damned military secret? I've been dialing for an hour. You can never get a cop when you need one. Balls, this has not been a Super Sunday. I lost my ass on the game. Goddamn Dolphins beat the point spread. Every one of my goddamn P's bet on the goddamn Dolphins. I'm coming down tomorrow."

"I thought you had to stay around a few days and collect."

"You got sand in your ears? I didn't lay it all off—I lost big. You don't have to hunt people up to *pay* 'em. They line up outside your door. Pete can take care of that."

"Guys from Vice aren't on your tail, T.?"

"Please, I have cut back on the bookie business since I am so busy with my new liquor store, but even when I was big, I was small. They wouldn't bother. No, but there's ice up to the testicles here. Been snowing for three goddamn days. I need to get somewhere where the temperature plummets to seventy-one degrees. I'll be at the Condado Plaza. Check the two dollar table."

13

BALTHAZAR BROUGHT TWO more cups of creamy white coffee into the Investigation Room. Here there was no distracting sunlight, only rows of overhead fluorescent lights. Nor was there the panoramic view of San Juan available to the officers and civilian workers on most of the upper stories of headquarters. Since this room, usually set aside for meetings, had not in the past been used every day, it had slowly filled with items no one else knew where to put. Boxes with small strings of Christmas lights and a crèche were shoved in one corner. Posters of Easter rabbits and the risen Christ leaned behind a file cabinet with missing drawers. Plastic chairs and boxes of Styrofoam coffee cups were stacked against one wall. The bulletin boards around the room had articles on the current case jumbled with outdated memos.

On a table at one end of the room there were overflowing metal in-trays, each with a taped label indicating their contents. All these reports concerned the three victims—

background information, interviews with those who had known them, status reports on this aspect of the investigation. The data on sex offenders were kept in the Sex Crimes office around the corner. The reports called in by worried citizens were in the small Homicide radio room in back of the glassed-in phone center in the front. Balthazar put one cup in front of Sixto, moved aside the huge pile of new reports to make room for his own, and sat down heavily.

"Who would have thought, Sixto, that there would be such an unholy number of people around that university who use a hyperbaric chamber?"

"*Sí*, all the oceanographers and half the medical school. The heart specialists, the tropical disease experts, the bacteriologists. Yesterday, I had never heard of a hyperbaric chamber. Today I am an expert on the many, many little things that will not grow if you increase the oxygen level. Or decrease the oxygen level. And never, in the entire rest of my life, will this subject come up so that I can display my great knowledge."

"No, Sixto. It's the other way around. Right after you hear a word, a phrase, a fact, you hear it again and again. Soon you will feel that, unknown to you, half the population of San Juan has been out there talking about hyperbaric chambers."

"Yet it is funny, no? I have been thinking and thinking about this man, and I never imagined him as a . . . scientist."

"No, and of course, he doesn't have to be one. All kinds of people wander around a university. People see them and simply assume that they have a position there. No one asks. Haverford was a student there in the past. He would be familiar with the university and perhaps the Oceanography Department. He could have managed."

"And he is a scuba diver, no?" Sixto mused aloud. "He would know about the use of such things, he would probably have seen how they are operated, might even have studied. . . ." His voice trailed off, and he shook his head glumly. "But Haverford, Lieutenant. We think this young man has a motive for killing his friend, the swimmer, Susan.

A crime of passion. Why then does he strangle the Torres girl first?"

"Agreed. But let's state the possibilities. *One:* The killer has no motive, or none that we can understand, to kill any of the three. He simply chooses them at random. *Two:* He has no motive to kill any of them, but he knows one or more and he chooses them because it's easier for him to lure them to a deserted place. *Three:* He has a motive to kill, but it has nothing to do with any of these particular women. *Four:* He has a motive to kill one of them and then, being a clever and ruthless man, he kills the other two to throw off our investigation."

"I have been giving much thought to number Three—" Sixto began miserably.

Balthazar looked steadily at the young man. "So has Chief Villareal. He is investigating Three. And One and Two. We only have to worry about Four. So do you think Haverford is a clever and ruthless young man?"

"He is very intelligent, but—"

"Not quite the same thing, is it? Then there's his friend, Rik Janssen. Background check shows his real name is Enrique Janssen, from Yuma, Arizona, but his mother has only lived there for ten years. He grew up in different cities in the Southwest because his mother moved around looking for work. The people at the restaurant remember Julian St. John having dinner there on Sunday, and they think he was with a tall man, but one with longish dark hair. I talked again to Janssen. Apparently he has a wardrobe of wigs and it just slipped his mind that he had been wearing a dark one on Sunday. Said he really prefers the blond ones."

"*He* is a skilled technician."

"I imagine the man who would kill this way as not only intelligent, but resourceful, viewing his own survival as the most important thing of all. A man who thinks quickly, acts without hesitation. We tend to think of people involved in scientific work as the kind who weigh all aspects of a situation before making a decision. On the other hand, we both are bothered by the uniformity of these murders, the almost clinical detachment of the killer. Perhaps we should have remembered the phrase: 'Beware the mind that measures.'"

Sixto looked at Balthazar in puzzlement.

"A line from William Blake, an English poet. My Aunt Gretje was a fanatic about reading. She'd *thunk* my head with her forefinger and say, 'Stuff your mind now while it is fresh. You will understand when you are old the meaning of what you read earlier, and you will be able to recall it all. When one is old, the memory of the day before yesterday is gone, but the memories stored in youth are ever present. Have something worthwhile to remember.' Thunk, thunk. She had a hard finger."

"You were raised by this aunt?"

"After my parents were killed, she moved right in. I was very young. She was my father's sister, and she'd never married. I don't think that she wanted to raise a child. But she was a duty-doer. The Dutch are made of stern stuff. A good woman. I miss her. But, back to the subject. If the Strangler is a well-educated man, he would be reasonably familiar with what pathologists can do. But he certainly must have assumed the body would be a skeleton before it was found. So did he just need to buy himself a little time? Why the hell put her body in that damned chamber?"

"That we know he used this chamber represents our first breakthrough. It is a real help. But I could find it in my heart," Sixto said, eyeing the paperwork with consternation, "to wish that he had just put her into a nice big freezer."

"God, yes. Or that that expert on tetanus had lockjaw himself. Five pages on why he has to use a hyperbaric chamber before he gets to when he used it that weekend. Turned out he had the wrong weekend. Give me that pile next to your elbow. This coffee is awful."

As Sixto handed the thick stack of papers to Balthazar, the phone rang. The voice of the officer at the gate in the downstairs corridor asked Balthazar in a pleasant soprano if he would be able to have a few words with Mrs. Hoover. Honno Gallo of the Press Relations Office had escorted her to a conference room on the east side of the tenth floor.

"Yes, of course," Balthazar agreed, slightly puzzled. He had read the woman's statements, taken when she arrived six days ago. They had not been informative.

She said in the interviews that she herself rarely saw her stepdaughter Karen. Their home was in Connecticut, and Karen spent even her university vacations in Puerto Rico because of her baseball schedule. Sometimes her father would fly down to see Karen, but she herself did not accompany him. She knew none of the girl's friends, nothing of her life-style. Her husband, she informed the officers, was under medical care because of the shock of Karen's death and unable to make a statement.

Gallo was alone, leaning against the marble wall next to the elevator when Balthazar got off. "I was just on my way to see you when I heard the lady asking for you. So instead of bringing her to your impromptu office—nice as that is, of course—I brought her here to the conference room. I must say the class of people visiting Homicide has improved since your arrival, Lieutenant. But first," he handed a sheet of paper to Balthazar, "I have spent a fruitful hour with the encyclopedia, writing up information on the hyperbaric chamber for the media. A monumental achievement, given the fact that I am allowed only to use words of one syllable. Could you cast your eye over that for correctness, O Resident Expert?"

"But, Honno, *I* don't know. . . . Far from being an expert—"

"Nonsense," Gallo slid onto the elevator. "It was a unanimous vote." The doors closed on his grin.

Pamela Hoover was in the carpeted, paneled room, looking out the window, when Balthazar entered. A magnificent red fox coat was draped on a heavy wooden chair next to her. On another chair sat a small, expensive leather suitcase and a matching purse.

When she turned, Balthazar's breath caught in his throat. The woman looked barely older than her twenty-year-old stepdaughter. And she was stunning. She looked exactly like one of the stars of a prime-time television soap opera whose name he couldn't remember but whose face was everywhere. Her platinum hair was swept back in a meticulous style that emphasized the oval of her face. Her earrings, necklace, and bracelet were of heavy gold.

She walked toward him, unsmiling. Her beige silk dress clung to her slim figure. One hand was slightly outstretched toward him, and in the other, she held a slim pair of leather gloves.

Balthazar introduced himself, took her hand, and murmured his sympathy.

"Pamela Hoover." Her hand was soft, her handshake only a touch. "Thank you for giving me your time." Her voice was as perfect, and as remote, as she was.

She gestured toward her suitcase. "I'm on my way to the airport. I'm taking Karen's body back, and I stopped in to pick up the jewelry she was wearing at the time of her death. Only earrings and one ring. But they are valuable. I'm surprised they were returned."

In one way, Balthazar thought, she was the exact opposite of her television counterpart, whose eyes had a tendency to widen when emotion was called for. Pamela Hoover's face was devoid of all expression. He wondered briefly if she had schooled her face to remain so still to avoid wrinkles. Even her voice lacked emphasis. Her only movement was an occasional abbreviated gesture with the gloves and a slight, but constant, adjustment of a large emerald and diamond ring so that it remained perfectly centered on her left-hand ring finger.

"My husband, of course, was unable to come. He is not a well man, and this was very painful for him."

Seated now a few feet from her, he could see that she was slightly older than he had first supposed. Early thirties, perhaps, more than ten years older than Karen.

"I read that you were working on this case. I was very relieved," she began carefully.

Balthazar said nothing.

"I want to be able to reassure my husband, you see."
She seemed unsettled by his lack of response. She looked
out of the window at the large U.S. Post Office across the
street from headquarters as if she were interested in its ar--
chitecture.

At last she went on. "I'm sure that there is nothing
either of us could tell you that would help in a case like this.
No doubt Karen was simply in the wrong place at the wrong
time. But he will ask. Naturally. In addition, one is not sure
how competent. . . ."

She twisted her gloves and then carefully smoothed
them.

"I have tried to arrange everything as my husband
would want," she continued. "He prefers cremation, so I
contacted a columbarium near our home and sent the obitu-
ary to the papers. The family lawyer has been notified. Under the terms of Karen's will, all her assets revert to her
father." She seemed to be ticking items off a mental list that
needed constant checking. "There was the memorial service
here for her friends, and her belongings will be shipped
back. In terms of . . . apprehending her murderer, perhaps
you could tell me if there is any progress?"

Balthazar considered the usual vague phrases and decided in favor of a question of his own.

"Did Karen write home about her activities? Mention
her friends, her teammates?"

"She rarely scribbled more than a postcard, and I can't
imagine that she would mention baseball."

He waited.

"You see, Karen's friends at home, if they are interested
in sports, tend to sail, and ride horses. My husband finds
that unfeminine, and Karen knew that. Those young
women who spend their time—and it takes a great deal of
time—being becomingly feminine, he considers useless.
Those who work in various causes he thinks are stupidly
idealistic. She may have hoped that an unconventional
choice would please him."

She paused, then added, "I think he found that what
she did—playing softball in Puerto Rico—was quite un-

usual and therefore rather . . . amusing. But he was not really interested, would not have praised her for making a choice of her own, or for excelling at it, I'm sure."

She waited and finally asked, "Why do you want to know that?"

"I'm trying to imagine your stepdaughter. To see how the murderer might have approached her—if he did."

"She was proud of her abilities, I think. She tried hard to do well, and of course one gets immediate unambiguous approval for excelling in sports. You can see your report card right away, so to speak. Given her father's attitude, that would have been important to Karen."

She lightly rubbed an invisible stain on her glove. He found himself caught by that movement, but he couldn't think why.

"But, you realize, I've seen very little of Karen since she was a teenager. I was even a little hesitant when asked to identify the body. But it was certainly Karen. She had changed little. I was surprised to see faint traces of makeup on her face. In the past, using makeup was against her principles."

"Did Karen resent her father's marriage to you?"

"I imagine," Pamela Hoover said with only the slightest discernible trace of mockery, "that she thought he approved of *me*. Is there anything else?"

14

"**B**ALLS, I AM IMPRESSED," MacAtee boomed over the phone. "First, at your total dedication—after six and still at the office? Second, that they knew where you were at SJ HQ and put me right through, and third, that they had the good sense to put HQ across the street from the baseball stadium. Hiram Bithorn Stadium is next door to the basketball arena named after Roberto Clemente, the well-known baseball player. I am now at Bithorn stadium. Given that fact—and that even workaholics must eat—stroll over and I will buy you a hot dog with my ill-gotten gains, which are FP—fucking pitiful. We can take in some of the action. The San Juan Metros lead the league, but those Santurce Crabs are mean, very mean. Meet you at the gate in ten minutes."

T., a red baseball cap embroidered with *Santurce Cangrejos* sitting at a jaunty angle on his head, was leading against one of the iron stanchions by the ticket office.

"They do things right here, Balls, you notice? Close-in parking, good-looking stadium, and most importantly, lots of little honeys in tight jeans selling stuff. I even like the missionary ladies in their white dresses collecting for good causes. You can give them some money, get virtue points, and then lust after all the hard bodies to your heart's content. I never knew a Latin that wasn't an ass man. You come down here and you can see why."

They moved through the iron turnstiles and then through a wrought iron gate and up the stairs into the stadium. The seat sections were red, orange, or yellow, and clearly marked. But MacAtee was so busy ogling as they pushed down the crowded aisles that at last Balthazar pried the stubs from his fingers and located their seats.

By the third inning and the third beer, he was beginning to relax. The mild air of the tropics, which seemed to soften everything else, somehow made the crack of the ball against the bat sound louder, crisper. T. was right—Hiram Bithorn Stadium was beautifully designed. From the outside, it resembled a giant oyster shell—one with sharply pointed ridges on its edge. But the lights were strategically placed all around the edges, and they soared on thin posts high above the half-circle of the roof. The crowd's roars encircled the posts and hung over the field.

MacAtee joined in the shouting with enthusiasm, leaping to his feet when a Crab headed for home, recklessly urging him on with an almost full beer cup. At the end of the inning, Balthazar poked him. "T., I would like to point out to you that you are yelling and stomping for the Crabs, you are wearing a Crab hat, but we are sitting smack in the middle of the Metro section. Some of the people around us do not appreciate that."

"Wrong, Mondongo-Breath. The PRs are good types. They like to see people take the really important things like baseball with the proper seriousness. Listen, the day after the U.S. troops landed down near Guanica, the PRs threw a huge parade. Day after that, they started playing baseball. And you gotta admit these guys are good. Man on third plays regular season for the Detroit Tigers. Lot of major leaguers come in the off season. Ah, I wouldn't mind spending the whole year down here instead of three months."

"You spend that much time down here?"

"Got my work here, too."

"How can you make any money? Gambling's legal here. Jesus, T., don't tell me you got some kind of other operation here? The last thing you need is trouble with these cops. They'll throw you in the White Bear and toss the key in the Atlantic."

"Balls, Balls, you have an evil mind. The nature of my work here is necessary and highly specialized. I lay on the beach and watch the pelicans. You ever notice they hang out in large groups here? Sometimes nineteen in a row. Suspicious, eh? One constantly speculates. What are they up to? It's not easy work, but someone has to do it."

He gestured to the beer vendor. "Four *cervezas, por favor*. The beer is great here, but they gotta get rid of these Mickey Mouse little cups."

By the seventh inning, Balthazar was totally engrossed in the game. The Crabs were ahead by one, but the lead had changed back and forth several times, to the noisy delight of the spectators. He stared idly at the player who was on deck. The batter was almost preening himself, straightening his cap, brushing off his uniform, carefully smoothing the glove over each finger.

Gloves over the fingers. Mrs. Hoover's leather gloves. Gloves. Balthazar grabbed MacAtee's arm. "A batter's glove—what's the inside like?"

"How the hell would I know? You were the jock in our crowd. Some kind of wash leather?"

"Wash leather—that's it! T., the Hoover girl was wearing batters' gloves!"

"After the game was over? Why, in this fucking heat—?"

"And the McKinley girl. Rubber under her nails. Scuba gloves. T., the *victims* were all wearing gloves. Not the killer, the victims were wearing gloves. So they couldn't scratch him."

"Okay, okay, so calm down. What the hell does that mean?"

"He *talked* to them before he killed them—he didn't just reach out from someplace and yank his arm around their necks. He had to know them. Or he at least had to be the kind of man they would talk to. These girls were all nice girls—well brought up—what kind of strange man would they talk to?"

"Well, let me think. They're at a university. Some guy says he's a professor, somebody dressed up like an official of some kind. . . ."

"Right, right, think like that. He talks to them, he maneuvers them around so he can get just the right angle. He *planned* to kill those two. He even brought the gloves. He knew just what he was doing."

"Yeah, but Balls, the papers make him sound like a crazy—"

Balthazar ignored him and went on. "But the first girl, Imelda Torres, had ridges below the knuckles. Maybe he shut her fingers in a drawer so she couldn't get her arms up. Was he just lucky then and thought of the gloves later? He hadn't planned on killing her. The others—he brought gloves. And she's the one he put in the chamber. There was something important about that girl. Torres is our link to him, I know it!"

"Balls, calm down. You're letting this thing get to you. You know what your problem is? You need to get horizontal, grab some Z's, crash, pound your ear, doze, get about 140 winks, nap, rest—get some fucking sleep! You look like shit. What difference does it make? You said yourself the cops know this guy had to use this chamber so it's only a matter of time—"

"T., I have to get back to headquarters. I want to look again at the interviews with the people who knew the Torres girl."

"Jesus, Balls, the San Juan guys will find—"

But Balthazar was already half way down the stadium stairs. Sighing, MacAtee picked up the half-finished beer and poured it into his own cup. He nudged the gray-haired Puerto Rican next to him. "That new relief pitcher. He any fucking good?"

"*No hablo inglés, Señor,*" was the nervous reply.

MacAtee repeated his question loudly in English, enunciating exaggeratedly.

The man shook his head, a worried furrow on his brow, and repeated in Spanish that he spoke no English. "Oh, shit," MacAtee said despairingly, "the only things I can say in Spanish are 'beer' and 'Where's the can?'"

They stared at each other for a long moment. Then MacAtee smiled, made a pitching movement with his arm, pointed to the mound,. and raised his eyebrows.

"Ah, *sí.*" The little man beamed. "*El lanzador,* Ramon Ramirez . . ." He responded at length in Spanish, peppering his sentences with references to ERAs, spitballs, and the *Nueva* York Yankees. Various fingers were held up to indicate statistics.

MacAtee whistled appreciatively. "Pretty fucking wonderful," he agreed, signaling the vendor to buy a beer for his new friend.

15

"MOST INTERESTING, LIEUTENANT. And you are un-doubtedly right about the gloves. It would be virtually impossible to trace a particular pair here, though. They would be sold in many sporting goods stores, as well as department stores. They are a common item."

He had been sorting the reports from the university into various groups on his desk top. He put them down, leaned back in his chair, and shrugged expressively. "But I am not so sure I would agree that this means that the killings of the Hoover and McKinley girls were, how do you say it in English, 'cover-ups' for the murder of the Torres girl. We looked carefully at that girl and her background. Nothing, nothing. She was only a file clerk in medical records. And we could find no trace of a close relationship with a man. . . . Although, of course, her car was found in back of that bar. Still, I think that merely means the killer surprised her as she was leaving."

"If that is true, we have to imagine him stuffing her body, say in the trunk of his car, driving some ways across town, transferring it to a crate or something, and taking it to the chamber. He does *not* hide the other bodies. It must mean something."

Villareal hesitated. "But he could not have known the other bodies would be found immediately. To look for this man's logic will not necessarily lead us to the answer, Lieutenant. To study his actions, yes; to understand them, no. He is adaptable, quick-witted. The first girl has no chance to scratch him, perhaps by lucky accident he has caught her fingers in a drawer. He thinks, 'I must remember that.' Next time he prepares himself with the gloves. But he may not be rational in other ways, you know."

"But you do agree that those gloves mean that he must have been at least talking to those two girls before killing them. And that we should look again at all the interviews. Particularly in the case of Karen Hoover. She was seen talking to several people, and that man who looked like a reporter—"

"*Sí*, Montez noted that, too. He went back and talked to the teammate who mentioned it. But her description was no better. The man was clean shaven, probably wore glasses, some kind of baseball cap. Montez asked why she had thought the man in the parking lot was a reporter. Did she know him from somewhere else? But the girl says no, she thought that because of all his camera equipment."

"But—" Balthazar started to interrupt.

"Now," Villareal said with a tolerant smile, "that may well help when we get these lists narrowed down. Otherwise, such a vague description. It would fit many, many men. You recall that Zodiac killer—the police have a description of him, too. But he has never been caught."

"Damn." Balthazar leveled a finger at the papers on Villareal's desk. "Somewhere in these reports, or in the trays in the investigation room, or in the radio room, we probably already have a vital piece of information. I know it has something to do with Imelda Torres."

"You are probably right, Lieutenant. But perhaps even by tomorrow we will have finished the interviews at the university. These must be done and gone over scrupulously. A good many people have already been eliminated. We will then be down to a list of possibles. But take another look at the Torres files. It is now ten and rather late to talk again to anyone. I would not recommend," he said tactfully, "awakening Mrs. Torres. She scolds us for twenty minutes every time as it is. She calls and asks for me personally. Not only does she tell me that all I am doing is sitting on my behind, she says that four generations of my family have only sat on their behinds. Now . . ." Villareal's eyes moved wistfully back to his papers.

Two hours later, Balthazar sat slumped at a table in the Investigation room. Rereading all these reports had told him nothing. Yet he had made a few notes and tomorrow he would go back and question Mrs. Torres. Maybe the girl might have said something about her work that was useful.

He looked at his watch. It would soon be Tuesday. Contrary to rumors that the Strangler would strike again over the weekend, he had apparently spent a quiet time at home. The press had pulled out some of their vans, and the crowds outside headquarters were dwindling slightly. Yet he felt no slackening of his own tension.

"Why are you here so late?"

Angel Negrón was lounging against the doorjamb and picking his teeth. His *guayabera* was freshly laundered, his pants sharply creased. Balthazar, glancing down at his own mustard-stained, rumpled shirt, did not reply.

"Didn't they tell you, Lieutenant? I have solved the case. You can go home. I was the lucky detective today who was here when a young woman reported another attack by the Strangler last night. Through my astute questioning, I established that not only had she escaped being killed in the struggle, she broke the Strangler's nose as well. Now all we have to do is find a man with a broken nose who has no alibi."

"What are you talking about? I didn't see that report."

"We have our priorities straight here." Negrón bent his toothpick in half and flicked it onto the open file in front of

Balthazar. "We would not bother the big man from *Nueva* York with our nut cases. We file them—under 'N.' Although this report was a little more original. Out of the last fifty reports, I do not recall anyone else saying that the Strangler had tried to suffocate her by holding her nose."

"By holding her nose?"

"*Sí*, she said he put his arm around her nose."

"Well," Balthazar said, sending the toothpick spinning off onto Negrón's shoe, "at least she got the method right, if a little high up on the face."

"Well, you see, our little victim was staggering along near the campus, having just left a cheery little bar. No, no, she wasn't drunk. Not she. Of course not. Although she was singing a little song and doing a dance step or two. But then, she drops her cigarette and just as she looks down to find it, a guy comes out of the bushes and puts his arm around her face."

"Did she have any bruises on her face?"

"A little mouse on the cheekbone, maybe. Her eye might turn black from that a little later. Probably," Negrón stretched, "her boyfriend hit her and she didn't want Mama to know. So she makes up this story about the Strangler."

"But," Balthazar said, "she did come into headquarters to report it."

"They *all* do, or they at least call into their local station. Otherwise, how could they get any attention?"

"Still, it's interesting that she said he grabbed her from the back. Did any of the other women mention that they were grabbed from the back?"

"Who knows? Who cares?"

"It *could* have happened, you know. The success of that method depends on the victim's chin being up. If she happend to look down at the precise moment, and. . . . How did she say she broke his nose?"

"She was wearing very high heels, a little off balance, threw her head back hard and hit him in the nose. Blood in her hair, blood all over the place. His."

"Did it get on any of her clothing? Does she still have those clothes?"

"You could check."

"What was the girl's name?"

"You know your problem? You're like all the other *gringos*. You can't believe we poor Puerto Ricans can do anything right."

"Can you remember the girl's name?"

"Maybe Diaz remembers," Negrón said negligently, turning away. "He took down the details."

"I'd like to see the report, Negrón," Balthazar said angrily, half-rising from the chair.

So look it up, Señor Front-Page." Negrón jammed another toothpick in his mouth and strode off.

16

BALTHAZAR SAT BACK down in disgust. He drummed his fingers and thought. He should look at that report. On the other hand, Negrón's assessment of the woman might be right. After all, Negrón was an experienced detective. In addition to the hundreds of calls from anxious citizens reporting suspicious strangers, unusual happenings, there were always the lonely people, often women, who came to the police. They magnified minor incidents into major attacks or made up whole stories.

And then there were the genuine incidents of rape and assault that had no connection with this case. Given the intense coverage by the press of the recent murders, many of the distracted victims were sure that they'd met the Strangler. Already-harried agents had to make quick judgments. Still, Sixto had mentioned Negrón's dislike of women, particularly those whose behavior he would consider not quite respectable. *He* would not have been sympathetic to that woman's story.

He himself could dismiss that report if only the girl hadn't described the attack as she did. Supposing she had not looked down just then? God must protect children, fools and drunks. Those superb young athletes, dead in seconds.

Balthazar put his head down on his folded arms. But that Torres girl. How could she have been a threat to anyone? She had access to medical records, but whatever information she had then was already in the files so. . . .

He was dreaming of running after a faceless man. There was a long corridor, and at the end a young black woman in a uniform was bending over a filing cabinet. He had to catch the man before he reached her. But this time, he could see more clearly what the man was wearing. It was a uniform of some kind.

But the uniform kept changing. First, a baseball player's outfit; then a referee's black and white shirt; then a soldier's uniform, but the rank was not clear; a police officer's with shoulder epaulets. In his dream, his leg was healed and he could run again. But he made no progress. The man was getting farther and farther ahead.

The man dropped his wallet, and Balthazar picked it up, flipped it open. It had official identification in it, but everything was in a foreign language, one he could not read. But he could figure it out, he knew he could, if only he took the time. A voice said mockingly, "If you can't think of the English for a thing, say it in Spanish with a Texas accent." But if he took the time, he wouldn't catch the man.

He sat up and rubbed his eyes, finally managing to focus on his watch. It was almost six. His mouth was dry and his body ached. He arched his stiff back and saw Stan in the doorway, dressed in a crisp white, short-sleeved jacket and tapered pants. She was smiling sympathetically.

"You look like a man who could use some coffee."

"Yes, yes, thank you. I'd love some." He blinked again sleepily. Sixto had said that many of the agents took advantage of Stan's efficiency, that she wasn't supposed to help

with their paperwork. But she could find that report. . . .
First, it was important to remember that dream.

Why were the woman and the man in uniform? Had
his subconscious mind picked up on something his conscious mind had missed? Maybe his mind was just punning
the way it did in dreams. He had told Sixto the murders
were uniform. T. observed that it might be possible for a
man in some official capacity to approach those girls. A policeman, yes, but the use of the hyperbaric chamber almost
seemed to rule out. . . . Still, he knew that some of the
agents had attended UPR before going to the police academy.

"Here," Stan said briskly, "this will get you ready for a
long night's day."

He thanked her, then, on an impulse, described the
report Negrón had mentioned.

"I'll get it."

"No, please, if you'll just show me where—"

"Sit, Lieutenant," she grinned. "You'd just be in my
way. You are guilty of reverse machoism. You'd let Cardenas
get it. Forget that I'm a woman and you have to be careful
about asking me to fetch coffee and find paperwork. It is
true that I do too much of that for this crowd. And that
attitude probably explains why, after thirty years, we only
have one woman lieutenant. But these guys are really hopeless at it. They're not just avoiding it. And I am a *little* better. It gives one great power. In the country of the blind, the
one-eyed woman is king." With a cheerful wink, Stan disappeared down the corridor.

Forget that I'm a woman. Everyone was concentrating
on the fact that the Strangler always chose women. It was
central to their investigation. But maybe it wasn't important. On a military base, young servicemen were often file
clerks, too. Imelda Torres was a civilian, a woman, and a file
clerk. Perhaps that was what was important. Something she
knew. As soon as Sixto arrived, he wanted to talk to Imelda
Torres's mother again.

He read the report, typed—badly—by Diaz. Certainly the
woman, Sandra Ortiz, had been asked many times, and in

several different ways, how she could be so certain her attacker was the Strangler. She was extremely positive about it. But Negrón was right. No doubt they were all positive.

Sandra had said it was clear that the man was not interested in just grabbing her purse. He could have slipped it off her shoulder on the run.

But suppose, she had been asked, he was a rapist?

She had thought that at the time, but during the night, she considered it and decided it was a foolish way to go about *that*. Surely a hand over her mouth, or why not put a knife to her throat?

It was the way he had done it, she insisted stubbornly. He had put the crook of his elbow over her nose and squeezed. Had she been a short girl, she would not have bumped his nose.

How tall was he? She made Diaz stand in back of her and demonstrated. Diaz was just under six feet. The killer, she was sure, had been a little taller.

Was he clean-shaven? She was not sure, the blood was all over his face when she turned around. And then he had immediately ducked and run. That too had given her the idea of the Strangler.

But a rapist would not want to be identified either, they had pointed out.

True, but he wasn't a rapist. He had wanted to *kill* her. Sandra was sure.

Was he dark?

There had been little light on the street, but enough to see that the man had light hair. Somehow he didn't look quite Puerto Rican, either, but she was not sure why.

And no, certainly not, her boyfriend had not hit her. She didn't even have one at the moment. And any man who hit her would certainly have very sore testicles.

That girl sounds believable, thought Balthazar, gratefully sipping coffee. Stan had said that the reports, which had not checked out and were assumed false, had not mentioned an arm around the neck. They had all specified hands on the throat, which is what most people thought of when they heard the word "strangled." It bothered him. He definitely wanted to talk to Sandra Ortiz.

Villareal was on the phone, and the conversation clearly didn't please him. He repeatedly asked the caller if he was certain of his information. At last he put down the phone, blew the air through his nose in disgust, and looked at Balthazar glumly.

"A professor has just returned this morning from a field trip with three of his graduate students. They have been gone since last Friday. And he is positive. He and several of his students had used the hyperbaric chamber last weekend. There was no body in it on either Saturday or Sunday of last weekend. And, you know, the pathologists agree that the body was in the chamber continuously."

He gestured bleakly at the neat piles of paper. "We start over. We will begin an identical inquiry on the monoplace chamber at the base."

"And no doubt," Balthazar scowled, "a lot of people there would have access to it."

"Yes." Villareal brightened slightly. "But they will have an accurate list of authorized personnel. No one just wandering around."

Balthazar had much less confidence in the efficiency of the American military. Someone walking along quickly with, say, a dolly and a crate, especially someone wearing a uniform—everyone would assume the man was authorized.

"Well, let's hope the number of possibles will be fewer."

"Ah, Lieutenant. But you realize that because we have here the military, all—every suspect—will have fingerprints on file! Every one!"

Villareal paused to enjoy the thought and then went on. "If the man has left even a part of a fingerprint on a valve of the chamber, we can then start building a case. We can go over everything he has touched. We can examine closely his car, his house, his clothing. We could even turn up a hair of a victim. With something this concrete, we can go over each of his movements."

Villareal sighed, this time with something like real pleasure. When Balthazar left, he was still lost in contemplation of the beauty of fingerprint files.

17

As they drove to the Torres residence, Balthazar swiftly filled Sixto in on the attack on Sandra Ortiz. "It's possible," he concluded, "that in person she sounds much less convincing. She works at the Plaza Las Americas. We can talk to her this afternoon. And while we're there, I want to send Alvalos some fruit. Stan says he's a little better and he's hungry."

"And my mother makes these oatmeal macaroons—"

They pulled up before the small white stucco house, jammed up closely to the neighboring ones.

"We'd better split up. Sixto. See what you can get from the neighbors. Ask them if Imelda Torres ever said anything that pertained to her work. A young woman who lives on this block, name of Magdalena Quintenilla, also has a job at the base. She's probably not there now, but you can check with her mother, see when she's due home. She's been interviewed. Doesn't work in the same department as the Torres girl. Still, it's worth a try." He concluded glumly, "I'll talk to Señora Torres again."

Remembering that earlier interview, Sixto hurried off with relief.

"I *realize* that we have bothered you a great deal, Señora, but as an investigation progresses, it is necessary—"

All of Balthazar's apologies had been drowned in fast-breaking waves of Spanish, denouncing both the total inactivity of the police and their constant presence on her doorstep. Señora Torres flatly refused to answer any questions that she considered foolish.

"You *Policía*," she reiterated, "spend your time with the wrong women!" Pursing her lips and puffing her cheeks, she shook her finger vigorously at him. Her dark eyes regarded him with scorn. Someone was baking, and the cluttered room was stuffy with the scent of roast pork.

"You see those *putas*, those street girls in their so tight pants, chasing after the men, and you think that all women do not know how to conduct themselves. And you, from *Nueva* York, you have no doubt the prejudices. Now, my Imelda, she looked like her father. He was black. As we say in Puerto Rico, '*El que no tiene dinga tiene mandinga.*' We all have a little black blood in our veins."

Señora Torres waved that idea away and sat up straighter. "But my parents had a piano in the living room. I was raised properly. By the nuns. And so I have raised my daughters. You *Policía*, you think. . . ."

In her indignation, words failed her. But only for the briefest of seconds. "Just because my Imelda's car was found behind a bar, you think she was in there drinking like a woman with loose legs. No-no-no-no-no! That man, he put the car there, I tell you. That *oficial*, Villaroybal or whatever, he is *estúpido*. No *inteligente*. He keeps asking me about the men Imelda knew. I will report him."

She tapped a pile of newspapers fiercely. "Now, these people, they know the truth, they know. They say the man is *loco*—"

Balthazar thought how infinitely preferable it had been when the poor woman was stricken dumb with grief. Or what passed as mute in describing the Señora. Finally, in desperation, he pulled his chair directly in front of her and clasped both the wildly gesturing hands in his.

"Señora Torres," he said firmly. "We now think that there is a chance that this man at least talked to Imelda before he killed her. Because of your excellent description of Imelda's character, which we do believe, we know that she would not talk to a strange man. So he must have been a man she knew at least slightly, perhaps a man she was helping at work."

"Oh *sí*, such a kind girl, she would—"

"You remember you mentioned several people Imelda knew the last time we talked. I want you to help me again. A man who would kill a girl like yours must be stopped. Imelda would want you to help us."

The tears ran down her cheeks, and she made no effort to take her hands from Balthazar's to wipe them away.

"*Sí*, she is looking down at me from heaven even now. Always she say I am too excitable, that I feel I must denounce the pineapple seller's great-great-grandfather to get a proper fruit."

"Now," said Balthazar, releasing her hands and handing her his handkerchief, "tell me again. Imelda did talk to you about what she was doing, and she may have mentioned something important to you. She may not have known it was important. But, to such a good mother, she would have told everything. So, repeat to me again the story about the girl she worked with whose husband refused to pay child support."

Dutifully, she rehearsed that story and several others.

Well, Balthazar thought, some of this had not appeared in earlier interviews.

"And then of course I told you—" she looked at Balthazar doubtfully "—about the poor neighborhood woman. . . ."

"Did she tell you that very, very recently?"

"*Sí, sí*. She was standing right there, putting her sister's hair in curlers, the last night I saw her—" Her face puckered in a round O of grief.

"Please, tell me again," Balthazar said quickly.

"Imelda said there was an officer she saw on our street. She didn't know him, but she'd seen him before. And Señora Alvarez, Avenaz, whatever, said her son, who had been taken to the States when he was a baby, was back here and had found her. But it cannot be of importance. The woman, she was crazy, and who wouldn't be, I ask you, given her life—"

"Tell me about this woman."

"Let me think. She move here with her husband a long time ago . . . twenty years, I think. *Sí*, Imelda was a little, little girl. I was still married to her father then. My husband, he was such a lazy. . . ."

She caught Balthazar's eye, and went on with her story.

"She was okay at first, came from Ponce, but her husband was an American. That I know. He was older, and not a proper figure of a man. Thin, you know? And thin blond hair on his head. He speak English funny, not like the tourists who come to buy my pineapples at the market. Slow. He even speak Spanish funny, through the nose. At first he was not so bad, but he couldn't hold a coffee cup without shaking a little. He began to say funny things, his wife was trying to kill him. . . . Then the shaking got very bad. He would sit on the veranda and you could see even from the street. Pretty soon, she kept him in the house all the time, but you could hear him cursing her, very loud. But she was a good woman. She always took good care of him. She say it was not his fault, and the doctors could give him no medicine."

Señora Torres frowned, tried to concentrate, and put on her glasses as though that would help.

"But then she stay in the house all the time, too. Hurry by without a word. Imelda, when she was a girl, would go to the store for her sometimes and even ask me to give her some old fruit from the market. After her husband die, she still stay in the house almost always. Just go to cash her check, and she just stand there in line, never look at you. Last time I saw her she look pretty sick, her skin funny—"

"What was Imelda trying to do for her?"

"She say that her son could get her proper medicine, put her in the American hospital. But that the woman told Imelda, no, he wouldn't help. She told him about his father, and now she didn't think he would come back. What kind of man is that, I ask you? But I say to Imelda that she should not listen. This woman is making up a story about the son anyway. She had *no* son when she moved here."

"But Imelda did say she had seen this officer going into the house and that she would talk to him next time she saw him?"

"She say that this man would have a lot of . . . a lot of something like . . . he was old? No, no, that can't be right. That woman down the street, she would no be so old. Her son would not be forty. Maybe she meant he had been in the service for a long time?"

"But you are sure she said the man was an officer? Now, I mean. He wasn't in the service before and now is doing something else?"

"I do not know. Imelda said he was not wearing his uniform when he was at the house, but she recognized him."

"Are you sure that Imelda meant he was in the military? Could he have been some other kind of officer?"

"What other kind is there?"

"Suppose a police officer."

"Imelda didn't know any *Policía*. You think she's the kind of girl who would be in trouble. . . . But she did go to school with that Ruiz boy—he is now in the *Policía*."

She shook her finger again. "*Mira*, that boy, when he was growing up, he was in trouble with the *Policía*, *siempre*. He steals cars. I remember this. And now, he himself is an *oficial*. How can that be?"

Balthazar sighed. "One more question, Señora. What's this neighbor woman's name?"

"Her name. I do not know exactly. We call her Avenaz, Davenaz, but that might have been her own name. Or her husband's name and it sounded like that. The only other thing Imelda said, I am sure, is that the husband had some kind of disease to do with dancing."

"You mean, *caused* by dancing?"

"No-no-no-no-no. Dancers are healthy, my Imelda said the exercise, it is so good for you that—"

"Dancing." Balthazar searched his memory. "Like Saint Vitus' Dance?" he asked doubtfully.

"No, that is not the word. Not at all. Like . . . like the steps you move. Like what Imelda studied. One person writes these little marks down, so the dancers know the way to move. I know, I know. . . . Ah ha, *coreografía*."

"Choreography?"

"*Sí*, maybe that's what you call it in English. I do not know."

She followed him to the door. "But see, this man down the street, he was not crazy like the crazy man who killed Imelda. No-no-no-no-no. That man could not strangle any-body—he shake too much."

"No doubt you're right. Which house is hers? I had better talk to this woman anyway."

"Now you are the crazy. You can't talk to her—she's dead. You are in the *Policía* and you don't even know who's dead?"

"You mean someone killed her?"

"No, no. Who would want to kill her? She was a sick woman, she die in her sleep. But no one knows for two, three days. The neighbors smell something funny. The am-bulance come to take her away."

"When was this? If Imelda were going to help her—"

"They find her the weekend I was so sick with worry because Imelda did not come home. And I told and told the police, called four times each day. I say something is very bad. They think she is with a boyfriend. Do not worry, she'll be home. They do not listen to me. . . ."

Balthazar left quickly. He would wait for Sixto in the car, he decided. On second thought, perhaps he ought to even move the car up the street. Señora Torres might have more to say regarding police procedure and come out to tell him.

18

AFTER FINISHING HIS interviews with the other neighbors, Sixto stopped at the Quintenilla residence. The door was opened by a pretty girl in her late teens. She had shoulder-length curly black hair, large brown eyes outlined with a great deal of mascara, a tip-tilted nose, and full lips. She was wearing very bright red lipstick, and a very tight T-shirt with the name of a rock group, Women At Work, across the front. She wore no bra.

She smiled at Sixto.

He handed her his identification, trying to look mature and professional, and asked for Señora Quintenilla.

The girl looked at the picture on his card, looked at him, and looked again at his card.

"Yes," she said with an even bigger smile. "That's you. *Agente* Cardenas. What do you want with my *mamá*?"

"I want to ask when her daughter Magdalena might be home from work. I need to interview her in regard to the Torres investigation."

"So you could interview her right now." She cracked her gum. "I'm Magda. But I've already been asked about Imelda Torres."

"I know," Sixto replied, "but I have a few additional questions."

"In that case, you'd better come in."

Magda turned, and Sixto noticed how very, very tight her blue jeans were. He followed her across the room and bumped into a chair. The chair slid into a tall, thin lamp next to it, which teetered precariously. Sixto grabbed for the lamp, and smacked his leg even harder against the chair. Magda giggled.

"Maybe you'd better sit down."

He took out his notebook and sat down carefully, looking grave.

"The man who talked to me last time wasn't very handsome," Magda said.

Sixto tried hard to get his thoughts together.

"You didn't actually work with Imelda Torres?" he began.

"No, she worked in Medical Records. I'm a receptionist." She examined her nails. "Her job was boring, but she made a lot more money than me."

"Do thay pay better if the job is boring?"

"No." Magda giggled again. "I've only worked there for a year. Imelda'd been there for *ages*. And they were training her on the computers. That pays better. She was always telling me I should get in the training program, too. But those computer screens, they hurt your eyes. And there's no one to talk to."

"What did she say about her work on the computers?"

"Well, let me think. See, I really didn't see her that often. Well, at first I did because she got me the job. Anyway, she told my mother about the opening and said I ought to apply. And at first I drove to work with her when we had the same days. See, I work weekends because you have to be there quite a while before you get all weekdays if you're a receptionist."

She paused for breath and shifted her gum to the other side of her mouth. Sixto was aware of an enchanting scent of attar of rose.

"But then I bought a car. Well, my brother-in-law gave me his old one and I pay him so much a week."

"When you drove to work with her, did she talk about people she knew on the base?"

"Well, let's see. If I saw one that was attractive, I'd ask her about him. You know, like was he married?"

"Do you remember her mentioning an Erik Janssen? Very tall, radar technician?"

Magda thought, twirling a piece of her hair around her finger. Sixto was entranced.

"Really good-looking?"

"I suppose so," Sixto muttered.

"No, I would have remembered."

"Did she ever mention a student named John Haverford?"

"All of Imelda's students were women, silly!"

"Did she talk much about her work?"

"That's all she did talk about. See, she was a lot older than me. She graduated from high school the year I started. She was in my sister's class. My sister's married now. So Imelda and I didn't know the same people. And we didn't like to do the same things."

"What did Imelda like to do?" Sixto asked, thinking wistfully that he'd really wanted to know what Magda liked to do.

"Oh, dance and . . . don't get me wrong. I *love* to dance. But she did that exercise kind. Not fun dancing. She stayed home a lot, talked to the neighbors a lot at night. Even the old people. And she didn't even have a boyfriend."

"Why not?"

"Well, Imelda . . . she was pretty serious and real straight. Well, she went out once in a while. But she never wore makeup. Well, maybe a little lipstick. She was always telling me not to talk so much to the men at the base."

Magda looked appealingly at Sixto. "But see that's my job—talking to people. And there's no reason not to talk to the people you work with, is there? Well, is there?"

"No, no, certainly not," Sixto agreed solemnly.

"Anyway, you want to know what I think? I think the reason she didn't go out much was that she really cared for Junior Ruiz. My sister said that even in high school she was always looking at him, talking about him. Now, you'll have to admit that he really is good-looking, for an older man, I mean. Still," she smiled at Sixto, "I like older men.

"And," she continued, "I saw him at the base a couple of times."

"With Imelda?"

"No, not when I saw him. He was with another man in a *guayabera*. An old guy—maybe forty. They were talking to a couple of guys from Security. So maybe it had some connection with his job. But she mentioned him a couple of times when we'd drive to work, I remember. She said she was worried about him."

"Why was she worried about him?"

"Well, she didn't know how he could afford that nice car. She said he had a Nissan ZX. I would love a Nissan ZX. I'd get a red one, I think. What kind of car have you got?"

"Not a ZX," Sixto said ruefully.

"Well, if he could afford one, I don't see why you couldn't. Unless you're married. Are you married?"

"No, no, I'm not married," Sixto answered hurriedly.

"So, you've been in longer than he has."

"In what?"

"The *Policía*. Don't you know Junior? Well, he only just started being a detective, I suppose."

"Ruiz never reported knowing Imelda Torres, or so I think." Sixto spread his fingers and ran them through his thick hair, lifting it off his sweating forehead. There were no trees on the narrow street, and not a cloud to block the enormous sun. The two men had opened both front car doors, but there was no breeze.

"Yes, but that could be perfectly innocent. She may have thought a good deal about him, might have noticed his car, but he might never have paid any attention to *her*. Maybe they only exchanged an occasional greeting. Why would he report having known the girl in high school, if they'd had no real contact since then?"

"Or," Sixto suggested morosely, "he might have seen a lot of her and has a reason not to mention it."

"Possible. She might have kept their relationship a secret because her mother certainly didn't seem to approve of him. She thought of him as a terror when he was a teenager, anyway. But it seems likely that someone would have seen them together and mentioned it. They've certainly told us everything else about that girl. And what could she have known that would make her a threat to him?"

"How he managed to get the money for a ZX," Sixto replied tersely.

"He would have had to tell her that and he wouldn't if he didn't trust her."

"Maybe he didn't tell her. Maybe she found out."

"But how?" Balthazar rubbed his chin and stared at the surrounding houses. Not only did they jostle each other, their gates crowded the cracked front sidewalk. But some were carefully painted, with immaculate white wrought iron over the windows shuttering out the heat of the early afternoon. Others had ugly cracks in their stucco facades; some had bushes so overgrown that the house could hardly be seen. "Her work in medical records seems an unlikely place to find out anything like that. She hears some gossip at the base? Puts two and two together? She tells Ruiz, or worse, confronts him? No, I don't like that. If he were in on some scam or other and she got the information that way, it would be pretty widespread. She wouldn't be the only threat."

"What about this work of hers with the computers?"

"Let me think. Magda saw Ruiz talking to security men at the base—right? Suppose that some of them have worked out a way to steal valuable equipment of some kind, and they need a way to get rid of it. Major league theft. Collusion all around. They enlist a Puerto Rican policeman to fence the stuff."

Sixto stared bleakly out the windshield.

"Now wait a minute. This is just a theory. We're thinking out loud. If we're looking for a motive, we have to turn over every rock. So, they also enlist a computer clerk to erase the records. If there's nothing to show that whatever they're stealing even arrived at the base, they wouldn't need to worry about getting caught. But Imelda notices something odd about the records."

"If she's in a medical division, *acaso*, a shipment of drugs?"

"Could be. But the reports indicate that she basically worked on servicemen's records. We'll have to find out exactly what kind of records she'd have access to. We will, of course, look for any sign of large-scale theft at the base. We can discuss it with Villareal. We can keep it in mind in examining the lists of personnel with access to the chamber. And we should listen to rumor. In an enclosed world like a military base, rumor is a good source of information. And," he added, "reports from the base are piling up right now, at this very minute, on our desks."

"*Sí, sí.*" Sixto flipped through his notebook before putting it in his pocket. "I don't think I got anything else new from the neighbors. An old lady down the street died."

"I know."

Sixto started the car. "First, I must go back to the campus to get the final report from that professor who says he and his students used the chamber last weekend. I have to get confirmation from each of those students. Sometimes I think that Villareal is a picker of gnats."

"Nits," said Balthazar, glancing at his own notes.

"Yes," Sixto said with feeling. "It will surely take the afternoon. I'll take you back to headquarters."

19

"SO NOW," BALTHAZAR said, crumpling his napkin moodily, "we get the authorized list of all the people at the base who used the hyperbaric chamber and work on that."

MacAtee reached over and fished a sautéed yellow plantain from his friend's plate and chewed it contentedly. They were finishing a late lunch at a small restaurant in San Juan's business district that specialized in Puerto Rican and Cuban food. He picked up the small bowl of red beans and scraped the remainder over his white rice. "These PR beans are good. Not bland, but not spicy. They put something queer, like pumpkin or a root thing, in them. I also like the Cuban black beans. Put little bits of raw onion on top, maybe a dab of sour cream. But they make you fart more." He swabbed the last bite of his rare steak in the juice and popped it in his mouth.

Balthazar could not be distracted. "Those chambers are not *that* difficult to use, T., and you know that someone walking around a base briskly with a dolly and a crate wouldn't be noticed."

"Would be if they were walking briskly."

"It's so damned time consuming and that guy could be ready to kill again. We're going to talk to the Ortiz girl at five-thirty. If I could only—"

"Balls, take it easy." T., abandoning his usual sideways glance, looked straight at his friend. "I told you this thing is getting to you. In New York, you're a cop, a good cop, but part of the team. You're too involved here. You're taking everything personal." He picked up a toothpick and nibbled on it. "I admit that this guy may personally be trying to kill you. There's some justification. What say the two of us hop over to the U.S. Virgins for a couple of days? Flights every half hour—take us twenty minutes. We could go to St. John and mingle with the rich. You could pick up the check. SJ cops be delighted to get rid of you. They wouldn't have to spend so much time guarding you. HQ is like Fort Knox now. Lady cop eyed me in the front hall as if I were a dangerous common criminal, instead of a respectable bookie."

"No, not now. All those people out there—they're scared. And those mothers, crying for their daughters. All that pain. And he acts like he's just swatting flies."

"Well, you said you believe that girl who said she really bent his nose. If that's true, he's gotta LL—lay low—at least until he heals up some."

"Yeah, yeah. But the whole thing is a lot worse than any goddamned jigsaw puzzle. You've got thousands of pieces and no idea which ones belong to the puzzle."

"If she's right, he's got blond hair." MacAtee looked around the restaurant. "That's gotta eliminate a whole hell of a lot of PRs."

"Yes, and if he posed as a reporter to get to the Hoover girl, it's very possible he's a blond. But he could have been wearing a wig. And some Puerto Ricans are fair, a number of South Americans are, and if he's in the service, he could be from the States. The field is too damn broad."

"Well, but then it can't be the queer, right? Too tall, she'd only have mashed his Adam's apple. And if he's got no beard, can't be the rich kid, and it lets out the guy you don't like at HQ. Terrible thing, Balls, suspecting one of San Juan's Finest."

T. stared at his beer reflectively. "Fun move, though. You could go around headquarters, asking the other cops if they didn't think the killer was one smart son of a bitch. That's kinda like what another guy who killed a bunch of women did. He wasn't a cop himself, but he'd go around to the bars and ask the cops on the case a lot of questions about the killer. Sympathize with them because the killer was so sharp, hard to catch. Hey, hey, now that I think about it, that's the guy who killed his mother, cut off her head, and used it for a dart board. You know *his* mother wasn't Irish. I'm still scared of Mom. She's mellowed some, Balls, but you know her. That woman is going to nag me to death even in the afterlife just because I use swear words and make book."

"You know, T., I read that a lot of those serial killers are getting even with their mothers. Berkowitz's mother put him up for adoption, but she kept his sister. That half-sister lived in Queens, and that's where he was shooting all the women."

"I don't think you can really understand the situation, Balls. You were raised by good old Aunt Gretje. If she were really, really mad at you, she'd sniff. That's all, just sniff. I sure miss her. She even predicted my future."

"She thought you'd become a bookie?" Balthazar asked incredulously.

"Sort of. She said I'd do well if I'd concentrate on my facility with numbers."

"She was envisioning a happy life for you at Arthur Andersen, doing accounting from nine to five, T."

MacAtee snorted. "She knew me better than that. You should just be grateful *she* was good with numbers. Sinking all your folks' insurance money into Polaroid in the sixties. If it'd been my aunt, she'd have bought Studebaker. You don't even have to do all this shit, Balls. You could go out there, lay on the beach, and look at the pelicans all day. But nooooo. . . ."

"Christ, T., those poor girls. If I could just imagine what Imelda Torres knew. . . ."

"If what she knew was in this guy's medical records, he'd have to kill every file clerk in the entire U.S. Navy and Marine Corps. Imagine ruthlessly slaughtering rows and rows of them. He'd be a very, very old person before—"

"It wouldn't be in his records," Balthazar said slowly, "if he was adopted and just found out about his past himself."

"What difference is it going to make? Once you're in, the good old Blue Womb has to take care of you."

"That's true. But say that what he found out was really bad, and he was paranoid about it. Say he was a high-ranking officer and that would affect a chance for promotion."

"I'll tell you one thing, Balls. Any high-ranking officer goes around the base pushing a dolly with a crate and it would hit the evening news broadcasts."

"The only thing Imelda was talking about at the end was that crazy woman down the street. Quite a coincidence she died the same weekend as Imelda."

"Every day, Balls, thousands and thousands of unrelated people die on the very same day. You want to know coincidence? I hopped in the sack with this girl in Vegas, and then I found out talking to her that I used to date her mother in high school in New York. Made me queasy. You know who her mother was? Janice Johnson, the one with the great pair—"

"Just think a minute, T. What difference could it make to anyone in the service if it was known there was an inherited mental illness in the family? One that sounds like choreography."

"Chorea."

"Korea? The country?"

"No, no, Balls. C. H. If you just listened to the right kind of music, you'd know. Woody Guthrie, one of the best, he had a disease called Huntington's Chorea. *Sixty Minutes* did a show on it. Turns your brain to mush, you get these serious shakes, and you get psychotic as hell. Scary as shit. His son Arlo had himself sterilized. But one sure thing—no

PR would have it. Group that has the gene are all Anglo-Saxons. A lot of them even come from the same area. The Guthries are from Oklahoma. Worse thing is you don't even know if you got it until you're older. Bad shit."

"Oklahoma. That's funny. I didn't put too much weight on what the language expert said, but—"

"Finding out about something like that could make you crazy, right there. And," T. continued, "if you were a pilot, they'd ground you, if they knew, I guess. But killing other people so they won't find out you got a bad gene? I don't know, Balls." Shaking his head, T. tasted the coffee the waiter had just set down, and then dumped three packets of sugar in it.

"A lot of people are adopted and they don't find out until they're grown up. When we were young, they didn't believe in even telling kids they were adopted, isn't that right? That Haverford kid would have been better off *not* knowing. Instead of feeling chosen by his adoptive parents, he feels that he must have been rejected by his real ones. He might be a special case. Of course, some of them know because they grow up in orphanages. Angel Negrón did."

"It is a serious waste that you have this great memory, Balls, and don't put it to a better use. I used to envy you because you never needed a little black book to remember girls' phone numbers. There I'd be, excited as hell, fumbling in my pocket for a pen and saying, 'Did you say two, three, one, four?' Come to think of it, I also envied you because a lot of those girls remembered your phone number."

"I have this feeling that when I go back to headquarters, Villareal will be chortling over the fact that we now have this list of only fifty people, and I'm going to be thinking there's probably only a few—say nine hundred—that aren't on the list, and in real life the reason the guy used the chamber was that no one had a clue that he could use it and—"

"No, no, wait a minute, Balls. We put all these nice pieces together and we have a blondish sailor or marine who maybe was adopted, knew one or more of the victims, comes from the Southwest, and has a broken nose. Now that narrows it down nicely. I think I oughta help you with these little problems more often, Balls. I got a flair—"

"T., I don't know about the broken nose, or where the guy comes from, but the odd thing is that particular description fits that sergeant who's always hanging around Maira Knight's house. He probably knew Susan McKinley, and he could well have known Imelda Torres from the base."

"Whoa," MacAtee said uneasily. "Let me just point out that you can't be accusing her other boyfriends of strangling women and get popular with the lady. And you sound like you want to. Let me buy you another beer—better yet, a nice brandy—and your head will clear and—"

But Balthazar's seat was empty.

20

"PROFESSOR KNIGHT, THIS is Lieutenant Marten. Just a couple of quick background questions. I hope you'll bear with me. I believe you mentioned that Susan McKinley met your friend Paolo, um, I've forgotten his last name."

"Davenport," she replied crisply. "Yes, she did. But I don't think he could tell you anything about her that I couldn't."

"Now, this will seem odd. But—" he thought desperately "—we have forms, very detailed forms, that we have to fill out on everyone connected with the victims."

He was intensely grateful that neither the note he'd received nor the language expert's conclusions had ever been released to the media. "You see, we've . . . um . . . heard from a man purporting to be the killer. Unusual accent. This must be kept completely confidential, by the way. So we're in the process of eliminating people. I knew that given your background in language, you'd have a good ear. If we

could just start with the men Susan knew in any way. For
example, do you know, by any chance, what section of the
country Sergeant Davenport was raised in?" He waited agonizingly through the short pause that ensued before she answered.

"Let me see, I know that he was quite unhappy at
home, and left as a very young man, went to California and
enlisted. Where did he say they lived? He still has a slight
twang in his speech. Yes, I believe he said he grew up in
Oklahoma."

"Good, good. And I believe you mentioned that he was
adopted? I'm sorry that I can't give you the full information
you'd need to answer these questions, but we appreciate
your help."

"I admit that I can't envision the reason. If there are
any other questions, I'd prefer that you ask Sergeant Davenport himself."

"We haven't interviewed him yet," Balthazar said truth-
fully. "It may not be necessary at all. Cross-checking, you
see. And, if possible, we try not to disturb people un-
necessarily. Especially with these meaningless questions.
We can simply eliminate them."

"Well, perhaps in this particular case, it is better that I
answer this kind of question at that. Paolo knew Susan and,
no doubt for that reason, talking about her murder is difficult for him. When I mentioned that you felt the Strangler
might have a motive, he became surprisingly vehement. I
imagine everyone wants to believe that the Strangler is a
madman, different from the rest of us."

"They certainly prefer that. Just one point. In discussing the case, did Davenport ever mention knowing Imelda
Torres?"

"That's a huge military base. As a matter of fact, he
brought the subject up once. Said he had never even seen
the woman. I would ask that you not bother Paolo just at the
moment, Lieutenant. He just called. He's had an accident
which seems to have upset him terribly. I—"

"What kind of an accident?"

"An automobile accident. He was rear-ended and hit his face on the steering wheel. Not really hurt, I guess, but he broke his nose. That's very painful, you know. And even minor accidents can cause one to—"

"Did he say he was coming over now? Right now?"

"Lieutenant Marten." Her voice became abruptly chilly. "I can appreciate that you have to be thorough, and have to ask—"

"Professor, this is important. Just do as I ask. Don't answer the door. I'll be right there."

"Please do *not* come over. You are surely exceeding—"

"Professor, I can explain. When I get—"

"Do not call me again! And do not come here." The receiver banged in his ear.

Weaving through the narrow spaces between the tables, Balthazar whacked his knee savagely against a pulled-out chair. He swayed; tears of pain sprang to his eyes. MacAtee, a few feet away, leaped up. Balthazar clutched the edge of the table and swallowed hard. "T., you've got to take me to Maira Knight's right now. That guy, he's the one. He's got a broken nose. And he's on his way over to her house."

"Balls, sit down, sit down, and let's talk this over." T.'s agitation was plain. "Theories are fine, but leaping to conclusions like this. . . . You've got a profile, but a lot of this is really shaky. Look, just because of Rose, you can't try to—"

"For Christ's sake, T., let's *go!*"

"It is four o'clock," MacAtee roared. "That means every four lane street has at least five cars abreast. Without a helicopter, and with luck, we'll be two blocks from here by five. How about this? Call your headquarters. Ask them to send a couple of guys over to sit outside her house."

"I did that. Villareal thinks I'm overreacting, but he'll do as I ask. They're just going to sit outside and delay anyone who is entering. And they aren't going to get there any faster than we are. Cars can't pull over to let them by because there isn't any place for them to pull over to."

"Okay, okay, we'll go. But for the last time, Balls, think about it. You go charging down her street like Teddy Roosevelt up San Juan Hill, and she's not going to let you in either. Ever. She could charge you with police harassment of her friends or something. Well, maybe I can explain it to her—"

"Listen to me, T. If I'm wrong, the San Juan police will think I'm much too excitable; Maira Knight will think I'm harassing her. But if I'm right, she's going to be sitting there, drinking coffee with a killer. A killer who is very upset, a killer who may say too much and then regret it, a killer who moves from thought to action very, very quickly. What would you do?"

MacAtee snapped his fingers. "A motorcycle. I'll get a *Tránsito* cop for you. Get outside as fast as you can."

By the time Balthazar limped to the street, T. had collared a man on a huge, gleaming, four-cylindered Yamaha. He was not a traffic policeman, but a scrawny little Puerto Rican biker with tight leather pants, his own weight in chains around his waist, a cut-off T-shirt, and a helmet sprouting ostrich plumes from the back.

MacAtee was screaming "*Policía*" at him, and the Puerto Rican, wriggling in T.'s firm grasp, was shrilly protesting in Spanish that he had done nothing wrong.

Balthazar pulled out his identification, and began a swift explanation in Spanish.

The biker stared at Balthazar's identification and then at him. "But Señor, you may be an *oficial* in Nueva York, but—"

In irritated desperation, Balthazar jerked out his San Juan ID and his gun.

The biker began to tremble. "But, you see, the traffic, Señor. I—"

"Goddammit," Balthazar rasped, climbing behind the man and shoving the barrel of the 357 magnum in his bare ribs, "Move, when I say move!"

"*Sí, sí.*" He kicked the pedal down and the motor roared.

"T.," Balthazar yelled. "Call Sixto. He's probably still at the Oceanography Department. He's close. Explain to him. He'll know what to do."

"Río Piedras," he screamed at the biker over the motor. "The fastest way."

"Oh Jesu," the terrified man exclaimed, but the cycle shot forward down FDR Avenue. He was screaming something at Balthazar, but his words were lost. Balthazar leaned over and shouted in his helmet, "And run that goddamned light."

Clutching him tightly around the waist with one arm, Balthazar could feel the biker shaking. But he managed to clear the intersection just in front of several outraged and honking drivers. They tore down the wide, packed road, weaving madly between the cars. The other drivers stared at the sight of a biker hurtling down the road with a well-dressed man hanging on behind. Bugle horns bugled at them. Burglar alarms were let off in sharp shrieks.

The biker turned right so abruptly on Highway One that the cycle almost tipped, and three pedestrians leaped back wildly. They made it through the next intersection, but ahead it looked as if there was not room even for the motorcycle to slip between cars.

"Go up on the median," Balthazar bellowed.

Again the man's protests were lost in the wind, but he dutifully sent the bike scrambling up on the narrow strip of grass. The median was planted with short palms and spiky cactus, and the cycle wove spastically around them. The palm fronds flew into the driver's visor, and Balthazar pressed his own face against the back of the helmet, the plumes in his nose. Just ahead, a fruit seller, hawking oranges from the median, looked up in amazement, then hurled himself on the hood of the slow-moving car next to him. They pounded down off the median and headed between the cars in the next block. A man, slowly and carefully pacing between the almost stationary cars and holding up packages of glazed doughnuts to entice the drivers, froze and then dived for the back fender of a battered Volkswagen beside him.

An amazed *Tránsito* policeman looked up from the traffic he was directing and headed back to jump on his cycle and pursue them. The biker slowed.

"Move, move," Balthazar shrieked, afraid of the need of a long explanation and then sirens wailing up to Maira's door, alerting Paolo. "Outrun him!"

"But, mon, you the *Policía*, ain't you?"

In response, Balthazar jammed his gun into the man's ribs, and his more powerful cycle soon left the sound of the *Tránsito* policeman's siren fading in the distance.

"Cut over to Ponce de León," Balthazar ordered. There was a bus lane there. As they turned onto the crowded street, the traffic came straight at them, but the buses were going in their direction, and the lane looked empty for a few blocks.

"There, there," he gestured with his gun arm. The biker tore madly down the bus lane.

Just ahead a bus was inching out, preparing to make a right turn. There was not room for them to make it between the bus and an oncoming truck. The bus driver, catching sight of them in his rearview mirror, meant to reverse quickly and get back in his lane to let the crazy cyclist by. Instead, he remained in forward gear and, when he accelerated, slammed into the bus ahead, which smashed into the bus ahead of him. The resounding crunch of metal drowned out the biker's wail, and even Balthazar cast a backward glance of despair. But he pressed the man forward.

Finally, they reached the top of Maira's street. As they neared her block, Balthazar shouted, "Cut the engine now, and coast." The biker was no longer screaming prayers; he had subsided into a defeated mumble.

Four houses before her trim white home, Balthazar hopped off clumsily. His bad leg throbbed. "Now," he said, sternly, "you get off the bike, walk it slowly to the end of this block. Don't look anywhere but straight ahead. Don't start that damned motor until you're all the way at the end of the block."

The biker, without one backward look, pushed his cycle rapidly down the street, almost skipping in his anxiety.

21

THERE WAS NO sign of movement around the silent house. A few cars were parked on the street, but Balthazar realized he had no idea of the make of car Davenport owned. Villareal had promised to send an unmarked car, but none of the parked cars had any occupants.

Had T. reached Sixto? Villareal had sounded unconvinced of the urgency. But Sixto would know. . . .

Balthazar walked up the path of the house to the left of Maira's. No fences separated the houses near the back—only a tangle of hibiscus bushes that he could crawl through and be directly beneath Maira's kitchen window. He wondered where Lena and the boys were. Would they be home from school yet? Did Lena perhaps pick them up?

It was very quiet. Perhaps he was in time after all.

He stooped beneath the wrought iron of the kitchen window, and immediately knew he was too late. A man's voice, high-pitched and intense, came through clearly.

He could hear Maira, too, but her words were muffled. She must have her back to the window. Her voice sounded soothing, calm, not at all frightened.

The man's voice rose. Davenport.

"Because of Mike, you understand that, Maira. All because of Mike. I thought that if he came back and there I was, never able to fly again . . . It just wouldn't be the same. Now I'm not a pilot like him, but I *was* a door gunner on the copters, and one of the best. Everyone said so. He couldn't see anything, streaking over those jungles. But I could. I could tell him what it was like, seeing those gooks shooting at us. We could talk about what we did. But they would take my flight status away if they knew. That's why I did it. I had to do it. I would be just a nothing sergeant, not a door gunner."

"But what *did* you do, Paolo? I still don't understand. . . ."

Davenport went on as if he had not heard. "He would lose all respect for me. And he *was* a friend of mine, you know. He wasn't like all those other hot shit jet jockeys who wouldn't speak to a non-com like me."

Again Maira's voice broke in quietly, but he went on without a pause.

"But see, Maira, I know now. I've known for a long time. I've just been kidding myself. Mike's never going to come back. He would have gotten out of any camp the gooks ever thought of making. Suppose he'd been hurt, maybe even hurt bad. As soon as he got better, he'd have gotten out. Even if he had to crawl. You remember all those stories he'd tell about survival training and simulated capture. I thought I was good when I went through it, but Mike thought of doing stuff I couldn't ever imagine. He was the best. Captain Midnight. He could have always escaped. So I know he's dead."

His voice turned accusatory. "And even you don't believe he's coming back anymore. I could see that right away when I got back here. All you think about's the kid. It's not as if it was Mike's kid, either. You say Rico's your sister's, but who's to know that? Well, maybe . . . but I saw how that cop was looking at you. That cop, another guy gets his picture in the paper all week, on TV, probably thinks he's a hot shit officer, too. With a little luck, I'd have done him, too."

"Paolo," Maira's voice was louder, firmer. "I realize that the shock from this accident has upset you, but—"

"You've got to listen, Maira!"

Balthazar crouched, paralyzed with indecision. Should he go back to the front of the house and see if reinforcements had arrived? If Davenport had a weapon, he could hold Maira hostage. Did the man care about her at all, or was she just a thing, valuable because of his obsession with her husband? Maybe he only wanted to talk. Whatever he did, he dare not alarm Davenport in any way. Balthazar, his stomach knotted from the pain in his bent knee, decided to stay where he was. At least he could hear. He could judge from what he heard how to react.

"That's right, please just sit down. Let me tell you. No one else here even knows Mike."

Davenport's voice was calmer, more controlled.

"See, when I was a kid, I thought about my name. Paolo. I thought my mother was Spanish, probably. Maybe even rich. Not like those goddamned Okies I live with. That old bastard, he'd beat me and beat me for the slightest little thing. I figured my dad would kill him if he knew. I'd lay awake at night and imagine my dad coming up the hill to that shack, pulling that door right off, kicking the shit out of that Okie devil, carrying me away. *They* said they were related to my dad, but their name wasn't Davenport. Sounds like an important name, doesn't it? There's even a town named Davenport near where we lived. Little shitty town, but a town. But they wouldn't tell me nothin' about my dad. I begged and begged Madge. She wasn't too bad, but she didn't care anything about me. And she couldn't do anything to help me. I had to go to school wearing a flour sack for a shirt. The other kids laughed. Said I had a spic name. And my dad never came."

There was a long pause. Maira said nothing. Balthazar burned to stand up, to see. Maybe Davenport had already killed her and was talking to her anyway. No, he desperately tried to convince himself, there would have been some kind of noise, something. Even if he could risk the chance of being seen, one could see little through the wrought iron and screens into the unlighted kitchen.

Finally the voice began again, inexorably. "Last year, when Madge took sick, she wrote me and I flew back to visit. The old bastard had taken off long before. I told her she had to tell me about my folks now, now that I was grown up. She said I didn't want to know. She said my dad was dead and I should leave him buried. But she did tell me my mom was Puerto Rican, that she wanted to keep me, but by the time I was born, my dad was already in a bad way."

Again there was absolute silence. A wasp zoomed past Balthazar's ear. He jerked his head and almost lost his balance. He leaned sideways, put some weight on one hand, hoping to ease the caustic strain on his joint.

"Now that made me feel good. My mom wanted me. Madge said she came from Ponce, and her name was Lilia. That's all she knew. So I came back here. I didn't want to tell you until I knew for sure. I was just going to show up one day, acting natural, and I'd be with this nice lady. I'd say, 'Maira, I'd like you to meet my mother.' I thought she'd be proud that I knew a lady like you, teaching at the university and all. I thought we could be like a family, come to Sunday dinner. And who knows, I even thought, if the worst happened, if Mike never came back, you and I could get married, have a kid. He'd be tall, have blond hair. See, it would have been like Mike's kid. Go to college and everything."

This time, there was no mistaking it. Davenport was crying. With a rush of relief, Balthazar heard Maira's reassuring murmur.

"Every week I went to Ponce and looked and looked at marriage registrations. Every time I told myself that this would be the day, the day I'd get some information and I'd find her, I'd find my mother."

There was a strangled little cry. "Well, I found her, I found her, Maira. Some lady, all right. Oh God, she had stringy gray hair hanging all over her face, and her eyes, they looked like dead people's eyes. Bugs all over the house, all over. She just jabbered and jabbered in Spanish. I was sure that *my* mother would speak English. But I understood a little, and a lot of it didn't seem to make much sense. Still, when I told her my name, she started to bawl and pray and kept calling me her son. She tried to hug me, but she smelled real bad. I kept asking and asking about my father. She started to snivel even more, and kept repeating this phrase over and over—she even said it in English. It was her tone, too, and the shit-faced way she looked at me when she told me. I finally left; I told her I'd come back. But she started to look hopeless. She wouldn't stop sniveling. I could tell she didn't believe me. I went right back to the base library and looked it up."

His voice turned high-pitched again.

"Maira, Maira. She said 'Huntington's Chorea.' I couldn't have been mistaken. You don't know how bad this stuff is. There isn't any cure. You don't even know if you have it until you're older. No cure. They just tell you not to have any kids."

"Paolo." Balthazar heard the tears in Maira's voice. "I'm so sorry, so sorry. Are you really sure?"

"Of course, I'm sure. I found my dad's death certificate! Would I have done what I did unless I was sure? I had to do it, you understand?"

"No, I don't, Paolo, I don't. What did you do?"

"As soon as I was sure, I went back. She's too crazy to lock the doors or anything at night. I just slipped in. And after all she did give me away, didn't she? Women can't do anything. She was asleep. It didn't take any time at all. I *had* to do it!"

Hearing that repeated phrase, Balthazar knew he must act now. Davenport, imprisoned in his terrible self-centeredness, even expected understanding for those cool, brutal murders. He would not get it from Maira Knight.

"Paolo, what—"

He shouted at her. "Well, she might have told the neighbors, right? I thought maybe she hadn't had the time or they wouldn't listen, crazy as she was. But she did tell the neighbors. She told that fucking black bitch at the base and *she* asked me, right there, if. . . . Well, I figured they'd never find her body. But, in case, just in case, I had to kill the others so they wouldn't connect—"

"Susan," an agonized moan low in Maira's throat, "Paolo, not Susan. You didn't, surely you wouldn't—"

Oh, God, Balthazar prayed, Maira, Maira, just don't excite him until I get in.

He'd have to go in the kitchen door. He'd have to take the chance. Maybe Davenport's back would be turned, maybe he wouldn't have a weapon. Balthazar prayed his knee would hold his weight. He lurched forward, straightened against the knife of pain that pierced his knee, and hobbled around the side of the house, gun in hand.

Lena screamed and came running toward him. She'd been bent over in the back of the garden, picking vegetables. "Oh my God, Señor Lieutenant, you frightened me. What—"

Balthazar heard the sound of something heavy overturning in the kitchen. Then a muffled cry that sounded like Maira. Lena looked at him in blank horror, spilling the peppers she had cupped in her hand.

"Stop right there, cop." Davenport's voice now sounded strangely serene. "I can see you a lot better than you can see me. And you better believe me when I say I've got a knife at her throat. A real sharp knife. So you put your hands up. High! That's right. Now throw that fucking gun as far as you can. Okay, keep your hands up, and walk nice and slow to the kitchen door. Get that bitch maid to come in with you."

Lena came closer, almost babbling, "Señor Paolo, Señor Lieutenant, what is the matter—"

Balthazar grabbed Lena's arm, pressing his hand over her mouth. "Be quiet, do what he says." Her body stiffened, then sagged against his.

"That's right. Do what the man says. Now look through the screen, cop."

Davenport stood behind Maira. Her hair was twisted in his fist and her head was tilted back against his shoulder. A knife glinted at her exposed throat.

"Now," the marine said, "real slow and careful, open the door and let the woman in first."

Balthazar obeyed, holding tightly to Lena for fear she herself would rush forward.

Davenport's nose was bandaged and his eyes swollen. He stood very quietly, looking almost relaxed. A man most at ease when he knew what his next action would be.

"Good, good. Now here's what we're going to do. Here's what we're going to do. How many cops you got with you?"

"None."

"Sure, sure, you lying bastard. Just happened to be paying a social call with your gun out. Wait, wait. . . . You might be alone, at that. You might have been paying a social call, at that. Just coming around after work like a horny tomcat. But then you heard something, heard me shouting maybe, and you come quick around the house with the gun out."

His tongue flicked across his upper lip. "Sure, sure, you couldn't of known I'd be here. I was in a bar only a few blocks from here when I called her. And you couldn't of known it was me, anyway. Not even the hot shit cop from New York could of known it was me. I wrote you—too dumb to take the hint. A bomb didn't even give you the hint. Some bright cop. Rico's smarter than you. The kid saw you at the hotel, with the gun on your boot, the day you came. He was there with Maira, and he told me at Burger King."

He had a slight smirk. "Okay, okay, that's an idea. Maybe you got another small gun on the other leg. Now real slow and real careful, you lift your trousers—one leg at a time. Okay, no more guns, no knives. You reach over now and pull that phone out of the wall. Harder," he barked, "we're not just unplugging the service."

Balthazar ripped the yellow phone out savagely.

"Now, just lean over and pick up that extension cord on the coffee pot. That's just fine. You're good at following directions. Probably could have even been a hot shit officer in the corps. Here's the plan. And I suggest you listen good, cop."

He pressed the knife slightly against Maira's throat. Immediately a thin red line appeared, and a drop of blood ran down the blade.

"See how easy is it, cop? Killed a gook like this once. One quick one right across the throat. He didn't even have time to make a noise. He was still grinning when he hit the ground. She'll be dead before you get to me. And you're a crip, anyway. Aren't you? And I'd still have the knife."

Maira closed her eyes. Balthazar prayed that she would not faint.

"The lady here is going to put out her hands. Palms together, arms straight. And you're going to wrap that extension cord tight around her wrists. Okay, Maira."

She opened her eyes and looked directly at Balthazar. Her eyes were filled with fear and anger, but she stretched her arms out. Balthazar did as he was told.

"Now, let's see. You're going to take little Lena here and escort her down the hall to Rico's room. Good wrought iron on the windows; you can't get out. You're going to slam that door real hard so I can hear it. Then Maira and I are going to go slowly and quietly out the back door. We're going to go around the house and get into the car. But if you hear one start, you'd better not come running even then. You won't know if it's the right car, and I'd hate to see you come running out too soon. Maira would hate it too.

"Now, move down that hall to the first door and when the two of you are inside, let's hear that slam."

Enraged with helplessness, Balthazar threw the door shut. Lena sagged against the wall, curling her arms around her chest, and sobbed hopelessly and quietly.

It was only a matter of seconds before he heard the gun explode.

He tore down the narrow hall, richocheting off the walls, through the kitchen, and out into the bright sun. Davenport lay face down, blood rapidly staining his khaki shirt. Maira was on her knees, looking up dazedly at Sixto. Cardenas was walking slowly, gun outstretched, still pointing it at the motionless marine. There was the sound of running feet down the side of the house, and Diaz and another officer appeared, guns drawn.

"Oh God, thank God, Sixto." Balthazar pulled Maira to her feet, running his hands over her head, her sides, fumbling at the cord around her wrists, and then saw the blood on her leg.

"Are you hurt, are you hurt?"

Her eyes were huge with tears. "I skinned my knee. He's dead, isn't he? And I've just skinned my knee."

Sixto was feeling for Davenport's pulse. He stood and looked at Balthazar blankly. All the color had drained from his face. "I saw the knife, I knew I only had one good shot under his arm. And I'm a good shot, *Baltasar*. I'm a good shot. I killed him." He turned away.

The dry tropical earth does not absorb moisture readily. Davenport's blood ran in rivulets among the brilliant flowers.

22

"THIS MAN," VILLAREAL mournfully tapped the report in front of him that Balthazar had just completed, "was not interviewed by us. A failure of routine."

Balthazar was so exhausted that his vision had begun to blur. But the homicide chief was being so insistent in his questions, so generous in his praise, that he made an effort to rouse himself.

"But really there was no reason that he would have been suspected, at least at first. Eventually, perhaps. He did fit the profile. But I'll confess I was beginning to believe that every man I met had those characteristics. Even the women looked likely. After all, Davenport was only slightly acquainted with one of the victims—Susan McKinley. He certainly did not know Karen Hoover. He had no previous relationship with the Torres girl. I imagine that she quite innocently stopped him and asked about his visit to his mother."

Balthazar stifled a yawn and groped for his coffee cup. "But then, as I indicated in my report, he had two real concerns. He had already killed the one person who definitely knew he had a genetic disposition to Huntington's Chorea—his mother. He had been counting on the fact that, given her illness, her death would pass without notice. The Torres girl's question raised the frightening possibility that the death might be investigated. And, he now finds that she may have talked to his mother, may know his genetic history. Worse, this girl is in the medical records section. Perhaps she would bring it to the attention of someone in authority. He would be denied flight status. This is overwhelmingly important to him. His self-image is threatened. You know, Chief, I wonder if subconsciously he felt that if no one knew about it, it might not be true. A form of denial. There's no question that finding out one has that kind of hereditary disease would rock the sanity of the most stable person."

"Ah, *sí*," Villareal sighed, "but he does not panic. He does not *behave* like a crazed person. Instead he acts immediately and decisively."

"Well, given the man's training, it is perhaps not so surprising. Davenport was schooled in survival. His marine unit was given the most rigorous instruction in swift, independent decision-making to save themselves. Like the Green Berets. It was necessary for these men to be able to do this. Perhaps he was even selected for that training because tests showed he could. At Professor Knight's house he was teetering on the edge of breakdown. Yet when I appeared, his instincts took over. He became almost cool, planning his escape. A very dangerous man. Without the slightest remorse, he would have taken any action required to get away. And the minute he was away from the house, he was safer alone. He would have killed Maira Knight immediately, left her body in the car, and disappeared. There is no question that Cardenas made the right decision. Davenport had to be stopped instantly."

Villareal smoothed the edges of his mustache, his hooded eyes fixed on the ceiling. "Where do you think he killed Imelda Torres?"

"Certainly somewhere on the base. It was late Friday afternoon. He realizes he must hide the body until he can remove it easily. He thinks of the hyperbaric chamber. He puts the body there and boldly drives her car out in the stream of traffic past the guard. He had to run the enormous risk that someone would want to use the chamber over the weekend and would find the corpse. But even if they do, there is no reason to connect him with Imelda Torres. Then he probably set up an alibi for himself for Friday. But he knew that the chamber would help disguise the time of death."

"And he was unlucky," Villareal mused. "After taking her body from the chamber, he puts it where it surely never would have been found—except for the accident of the return of the surveying crew. Perhaps a year from now when the bridge was nearing completion, her skeleton might have turned up. But even a week later, when the land crabs, the birds, the insects, the rats had destroyed the flesh, he would have been much safer. Because of the broken neck, we would perhaps have seen it as the work of the Strangler, but we would have been unable to discover the timing."

"It was sheer bad luck," Balthazar agreed. "But Davenport was extremely resourceful. He decided to disguise that murder even further. He would kill two more women. What bothered both Cardenas and me was the killer's detachment. For Davenport, these murders were merely an exercise in self-preservation. So he was able to plan coldly and efficiently, destroying all evidence, disposing of the girls' clothing, covering his traces.

"As for his choices of victims, I think the fact that the McKinley girl admired him, would have been willing to meet him anywhere, made him think of her. Then, since she was a student, he chose another student. I'm convinced he stopped Karen Hoover after the game, congratulated her on ending her batting slump, told her he wanted some pictures of her for a newspaper. He needed poses of her in a batting stance. She showers, puts on makeup, gets ready for the photos. Then she reappears, probably excited at the thought of the publicity. But she has no bat. At this point he doesn't lose his head—sends her back for one. But he must have been sweating. Then he gets her to try on the gloves. Fusses about a bit. Gets behind her."

Balthazar grimaced at the thought. "But he has a good plan. He figured, quite rightly, that as long as everyone's attention was focused on the university and away from the base, it was unlikely that his own motive would be discovered. Even if someone had seen him talking to Imelda Torres at the base, it would not have endangered him."

"We did as he wanted," Villareal sighed. "We went directly to the university."

"Well," Balthazar responded, "but it was only a starting place for us. We would have broadened our search."

"But here," Villareal tapped another pile of papers, "is the list of personnel trained in the use of the hyperbaric chamber and another list of those authorized to use it. His name does not appear on either list. His commanding officer speculates that Davenport learned its operation at Camp Pendleton near San Diego, where he was previously stationed. The man's records show a high mechanical ability. I do not think his name would have come up in our investigations."

Villareal shook his head. "No, it was your careful construction of your own profile of the man, Lieutenant, and your promptness in acting on it that solved this case. The man might have gone on killing, if only as a response to our discovery of the link with the base."

"But it was luck, too," Balthazar insisted. "Extreme good luck for Sandra Ortiz that his attempt to kill her failed. She gave us the vital piece of information—that she had marked him."

"But that is the amazing thing! What made you believe her?"

Balthazar thought quickly. He did not want to admit that it was Angel Negrón's refusal to believe Sandra Ortiz that had intensified his own desire to accept the girl's story.

"It was your team's excellent collection of reports that enabled me to fasten on her, sir."

Villareal rose and beamed. In the chief's rare, delighted smile, Balthazar could see the vast relief. The killer was caught, and he had been an outsider with no connection to the Casera case. "I wish to shake your hand, Lieutenant. Both the Secretary of Justice and I appreciate your praise of our *Policía* in your first statement to the press. Of course, he wishes to release more details from your report in his early conference for the morning news. Also, he wishes you to appear with him at noon for the evening news. But now, you should get some rest."

"Thank you. Sixto Cardenas must come to the conference. He's the real hero."

As Balthazar turned the corner to leave the Homicide Department, he almost bumped into Negrón, who had paused in the narrow corridor to light a thin, dark cigar. He was blocking the way, but he remained standing there, slowly shaking out a wooden match. "Congratulations," he said sardonically, "you are a lucky man."

"I am," Balthazar returned evenly. "Getting Cardenas for a partner was a stroke of fortune."

"Cardenas is a fool. Shooting under those circumstances, he risks a charge of murder himself. And our citizens' gratitude lasts only as long as tomorrow's headlines."

He watched Balthazar, his eyes narrowed against the smoke. "You took quite a chance yourself, Lieutenant, acting so . . . how shall I put it . . . impulsively on very little information."

Balthazar fixed his own eyes coldly on Negrón's blank ones. "Ah, but it was information I got from you."

Negrón's eyes flared in anger, but he hid it quickly by inspecting the cigar. He flicked the small ash insolently. "So, when are you going back to New York?"

A massive hand reached out from the darkened doorway next to them and deftly whipped the cigar from Negrón's hand. Montez moved ponderously out into the corridor between them, and stepped carefully on the cigar. "No smoking area, Negrón," he remarked quietly. "Come with me, Lieutenant."

Preceding Balthazar down the hallway, he said without turning, "The reporters are all waiting for you. And it is not only the island press. The big networks from the States have sent their people here."

Balthazar stared at Montez's back in horror.

Montez pushed the elevator button, and glanced up at the floor indicator. "However," he added imperturbably, "I have a closed van waiting by the side entrance."

23

THE NEXT MORNING Balthazar arrived to find the department walls festooned with newspapers. Every front page
carried photos of him and of Sixto. Sixto was studying one
with dismay.

"*Mira*, they describe us as bloodhounds," he quoted
from the copy," "'relentlessly tracking down the monster
that terrified our city.' I look more like a Puerto Rican Terrier."

The photographer had caught Sixto emerging from a
police car. He had thrown up his hand to block the camera
flash in his eyes. He was squinting, and his mouth was
partly open. He did look as if he were snarling.

"Look at the one of me. It should make you feel better."
In the front page photo, Balthazar stood stiffly in front of a
microphone, and the Secretary of Justice, immaculately
groomed, had his hand on Balthazar's shoulder as if he were
detaining him. He himself was rumpled, unshaven, and his
hands were clasped in front of him as if he were handcuffed.

Juxtaposed with these photos was a service picture of Sergeant Paolo Davenport. Handsome in his uniform, he was looking alertly at the camera.

Stan came in bearing a hand-lettered poster, which she carefully taped under the pictures. It read: ATTENTION ALL POLICIA: WHICH ONE OF THESE THREE MEN WOULD YOU ARREST?

The phone rang and she reached for it. She held the receiver out questioningly. "For you, Lieutenant. Señora Knight."

Balthazar took the phone with relief. He had phoned her home, and there had been no answer.

"I wanted to call and thank you, Lieutenant." She sounded remote, even impersonal.

"As the police were leaving, I saw the enormous crowd outside of my house. Lena and I took the boys and our toothbrushes and went to some friends of mine in Hato Rey. That's where I am now. At the home of Carlos Santiago and his wife, Estella."

She cleared her throat. "I realize that this is really irrational, but I'm thinking of moving. Carlos says there's a vacant house near the university. A visiting professor from South America just left. The house is quite large, and well, we'd been feeling a little cramped at our house for a long time. Lena will miss her garden, but this one also has a large yard. . . . I just don't want to go back."

"I can understand, Professor. I tried to call you. To see how you were. In fact, I wanted to stop by, but probably seeing me will cause you further pain—"

"It invariably happens, Lieutenant. *Every* time someone saves my life, I have this overwhelming desire never to see him again."

But the brief laughter left her voice. "Somehow I blame myself for not suspecting more. Given the way Paolo always went on about Mike, I should have realized he had . . . well, a reality shortage. I guess as we grow older, we all try to recreate our families. This time we try to do it nearer to the heart's desire. We all fail at it. Sometimes we just make different mistakes. But Paolo never had a real model to start with—only a fantasy. And he had terribly high expectations; they would never have accorded with the way things are—"

"You couldn't have known. You couldn't have."

"That's why I really called, I think. So you would say exactly that," she said, pausing slightly. "More importantly, I want to thank you in person. I would like to take you to dinner. Since you're so famous, we'll have to come in disguise. Meet me at La Zaragozana in Old San Juan at dusk. Precisely. I'll be the man at the back table wearing a brown wool overcoat and a slouch hat. I'll be drinking absinthe and smoking two cigarettes."

As he hung up, he was smiling broadly. He caught Sixto's eye.

"She's recovering."

Sixto smiled, too, but Balthazar noticed he still looked a little pale. "My mother was so busy calling relatives and talking to the neighbors this morning that she let Cousin Ida fix my breakfast. I only had to eat *three* eggs." His voice was shaky.

Balthazar looked down at the desk. He tried to think how to tell Sixto how grateful he was. That Sixto was the best shot and the best partner. Here we are two men—sharing two languages—and I can't tell him. . . .

He cleared his throat. "Did you have a chance yet to read my report?"

Sixto turned. "I read it with much interest. I was happy to learn that we solved this case together using our investigative training, our experience, our reasoning, our logic. Of course, I was amazed to discover that the Sixto Cardenas referred to was *me*."

Balthazar grinned back. "Working with an experienced detective like me, Sixto, you learn that that is how it is done. One must depend on routine, rely on facts. You cannot solve cases using intuition."

"Never," Sixto agreed solemnly.

Stan came back, brandishing a telegram.

It was from Captain Helmsley in New York. It read:
CONGRATULATIONS STOP CONSIDER PREVIOUS INSTRUC-

TIONS REVOKED STOP BEFORE RETURN IN JUNE SOLVE ALL CRIME ON ISLAND STOP APPRECIATE SOME ATTENTION TO ASSIGNED CASE STOP

He handed it to Sixto.

"He means this? You're to stay until June? I am very happy that you will be here, Lieutenant."

"*Baltasar*," said Balthazar.

ABOUT THE AUTHOR

M. J. ADAMSON lives in Colorado and Puerto Rico.

☐ 25789-7 **JUST ANOTHER DAY IN PARADISE,**
Maxwell $2.95

Fiddler has more money than he knows what to do with, he's tried about everything he'd ever thought of trying and there's not much left that interests him. So, when his ex-wife's twin brother disappears, when the feds begin to investigate the high-tech computer company the twin owns, and when Fiddler finds himself holding an envelope of Russian-cut diamonds, he decides to get involved. Is his ex-wife's twin selling high-tech information to the Russians?

☐ 25809-5 **THE UNORTHODOX MURDER OF**
RABBI WAHL, Telushkin $2.95

Rabbi Daniel Winter, the young host of the radio talk show "Religion and You," invites three guests to discuss "Feminism and Religion." He certainly expects that the three women, including Rabbi Myra Wahl, are likely to generate some sparks . . . What he doesn't expect is murder.

☐ 25717-X **THE BACK-DOOR MAN,** Kantner $2.95

Ben Perkins doesn't look for trouble, but he isn't the kind of guy who looks the other way when something comes along to spark his interest. In this case, it's a wealthy widow who's a victim of embezzlement and the gold American Express card she gives him for expenses. Ben thinks it should be fun; the other people after the missing money are out to change his mind.

☐ 26061-8 **"B" IS FOR BURGLAR,** Grafton $3.50

"Kinsey is a refreshing heroine."—*Washington Post Book World*

"Kinsey Millhone . . . is a stand-out specimen of the new female operatives." —*Philadelphia Inquirer*

[Millhone is] "a tough cookie with a soft center, a gregarious loner." —*Newsweek*

What appears to be a routine missing persons case for private detective Kinsey Millhone turns into a dark tangle of arson, theft and murder.

Look for them at your bookstore or use the coupon below:

50 YEARS OF GREAT AMERICAN MYSTERIES FROM BANTAM BOOKS

Stuart Palmer

"Those who have not already made the acquaintance of Hildegarde Withers should make haste to do so, for she is one of the world's shrewdest and most amusing detectives."
—*New York Times*
May 6, 1934

- ☐ 25934-2 THE PUZZLE OF THE SILVER PERSIAN (1934) $2.95
- ☐ 26024-3 THE PUZZLE OF THE HAPPY HOOLIGAN (1941) $2.95

Featuring spinster detective Hildegarde Withers

Craig Rice

"Why can't all murders be as funny as those concocted by Craig Rice?"
—*New York Times*

- ☐ 26345-5 HAVING WONDERFUL CRIME $2.95

"Miss Rice at her best, writing about her 3 favorite characters against a delirious New York background."
—*New Yorker*

- ☐ 26222-X MY KINGDOM FOR A HEARSE $2.95

"Pretty damn wonderful!"   —*New York Times*

Barbara Paul

- ☐ 26234-3 RENEWABLE VIRGIN (1985) $2.95

"The talk crackles, the characters are bouncy, and New York's media world is caught with all its vitality and vulgarity."
—*Washington Post Book World*

- ☐ 26225-4 KILL FEE (1985) $2.95

"A desperately treacherous game of cat-and-mouse (whose well-wrought tension is heightened by a freakish twist that culminates in a particularly chilling conclusion." —*Booklist*

For your ordering convenience, use the handy coupon below:

The Mystery Is Revealed
Barbara Vine *is* Ruth Rendell
and Bantam is bringing you her haunting novel
of psychological suspense in July 1986

A Dark-Adapted Eye

☐ (05143-1 • $14.95)

Here is the stunning first novel by one of the greatest
living practitioners of the British mystery: Ruth Rendell
writing for the first time under the pseudonym of
Barbara Vine. In this chilling novel, a once adoring
niece delves into her family's psyche to uncover the
circumstances surrounding her aunt's crime of murder,
for which she was hanged. Sifting through layers of time-
honored illusion, Faith Severn must come to see her
family in a different light, recognizing how suffocating
affection can become twisted into something deadly.

☐ 25968-7   NO MORE DYING THEN $3.50
☐ 25969-5   A SLEEPING LIFE $3.50
☐ 25970-9   SHAKE HANDS FOREVER $3.50

Look for them at your bookstore or use the coupon below: